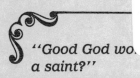

"Good God wo... ...ke me for a saint?"

"No, I took you for a gentleman!" she snipped, and turned to leave.

Renfrew reached out and grabbed her wrist to stop her. He told himself he was doing it for Romeo, but lurking at the bottom of his heart, unexamined, was a different reason. The stab of anger and regret at her curt dismissal was not the reaction of a mere interested observer.

"I don't have a mistress," he said angrily.

Jane studied him for a moment. He watched, bewitched as her scowl turned slowly to a smile. "You might have told me so, James," she said, and laughed.

LOVER'S QUARRELS

Joan Smith

FAWCETT CREST • NEW YORK

A Fawcett Crest Book
Published by Ballantine Books
Copyright © 1989 by Joan Smith

Library of Congress Catalog Card Number: 89-91216

ISBN 0-449-21636-5

Manufactured in the United States of America

First Edition: September 1989

Lovers' quarrels are the renewal of love.

Terence, *Andria* (The Lady of Andros)

Chapter One

ISS MUNCH looked around the crowded little bedchamber and shook her snuff-brown head. She was small in stature, rather grim of face, rudely outspoken, and as faithful as a star to her young mistress. "This is almost worse than being back at the Hall with your uncle, Miss Halsey. How a human bean's supposed to keep the place tidy when the room's not big enough to hold your wardrobe, let alone yourself and Missie, I'm sure *I* don't know."

"The room is certainly snug," Miss Halsey admitted. Its snugness at times caused a sensation of suffocation. The desk was rammed tight against the dresser, and it was impossible to open the door to the hall when the wardrobe door was ajar. But one became accustomed to a little crowding. Aunt Hermione had made some efforts at beautifying the room. The walls were covered in new flower-spangled paper, and the window hangings of green raw silk were unexceptionable. In any case, it was better than remaining at Halsey Hall with Uncle Horace. Anything was better than that!

"Belle and I don't mind sharing the bed," Miss Halsey continued, "and as to our trunks, you might as well put our party gowns and riding habits back in them and have them taken to the attics. We shan't be needing them, and they are cluttering up the hall abominably."

"We'll see about that," Miss Munch declared, fire in her eyes. "You're out of mourning now. You've been presented at Court, and Missie, too, as far as making her curtsy to the Queen goes. A pity she couldn't have enjoyed her Season."

"I do feel sorry for Belle," Miss Halsey admitted. "I had my crack at the beaux, but poor Belle was killed in covert. So pretty, she might have made a grand match if her Season hadn't been cut short by Papa's illness. And now that Papa is dead and Uncle Horace lording it over the Hall, a match would be so welcome. But not the match Uncle had in mind, of course."

Miss Munch snorted. "If you can call a sixty-year-old relic a match for our Missie. May and December is nothing to it. Swaddling clothes and a shroud is more like it. She barely eighteen, and that old bleater of a Rankin as bald as a billiard ball. Shocking, I call it."

"I daresay Uncle Horace thought it for the best," Miss Halsey said doubtfully. "Mr. Rankin has a good character, and an excellent bank account. My uncle is such a hermit, he could not become accustomed to having two ladies around the place. It was kind of Aunt Hermione to rescue us. She has no excess of funds herself, you must know, Munch. We are inconveniencing her terribly. This room used to be her son's study."

Miss Munch leveled a patronizing stare on the desk. "We could move that piece of lumber out. Mr. Pettigrew won't need it now that he's through learning. That'd give us room to swing a kitten. I shan't say cat, for it wouldn't be true," she added, mentally measuring the oaken desk.

Miss Haley considered this suggestion. "It's nice to have the desk, though. We have plenty of letters to write to friends back home. Let us leave it for now. I dislike to be forever bothering Aunt Hermione about shifting things from here to there."

Miss Munch continued staring at the large desk. "Why people who live in a shoebox must want furnishings to fit a palace is above and beyond me. Has your aunt seen better days, Miss Halsey?"

"Oh, yes. Like us, she is down on her luck at present. Her husband's early death left them high and dry. But Basil, her son, is looking for a position now that he has finished university. That will ease matters. And meanwhile the interest on my dot is more than enough to pay for Belle's and my own support, so we are no financial burden at least."

"I can live on less than you pay me," Miss Munch said at once. "I don't have to pretend to *you* that I'm a real lady's maid. Hot out of the kitchen I came to you, for I'd not stay on with that old scholar of a Horace Halsey, not if he paid me in gold bunions. Expecting us to eat cods' heads and pigs' tails and calves' feet, and never a slice of good-grained meat, fish, or fowl on the table. A human bean's got her needs, same as anyone else."

Miss Munch enjoyed the distinction of being a human bean. She spoke of it often; her criterion for proper conduct toward herself was whether that conduct upheld the dignity of the human bean. She demanded no less for her charges, the Misses Halsey, of Halsey Hall in West Sussex. No matter if they were all reduced to battening themselves on the late Mrs. Halsey's sister—they were human beans, and would be treated accordingly.

"We are not quite so purse-pinched as that, Munch," Miss Halsey assured her. "We can afford your wages."

Miss Munch nodded in satisfaction. She knew to a penny how her mistress was situated financially. Ten thousand pounds was the dowry she inherited from her mother. Safely invested in the funds, it gave Jane five hundred a year. Miss Belle had not a sou to her name, and old Horace Halsey had inherited everything else in sight—Hall, furnishings, cattle and carriages, income . . . the lot. The old nip-cheese hadn't even the grace to give the girls their own mounts to take with them to London. In revenge, Miss Munch had given their saddles to the church jumble sale.

"Well, if you're tight, just put my wages on tick," she offered, and meant it.

"Goose! How would you pay for your own personal necessities if I did?"

"What necessities would the likes of me have?" Miss Munch demanded, in a purely rhetorical spirit. "If I ever need money, well—we'll burn *that* bridge when we come to it."

Miss Halsey smiled ruefully. "We're good at that, are we not?"

"What choice was left to you? I'd not trust Horace Halsey, not with a ten-foot pole. Now don't be blaming yourself for this quagmire you've sunk us into by ripping up at your uncle. We couldn't have little Missie shackled to an ancient. She'll nab the handsomest *parti* in town, once the lads get a look at her. She's pretty as a pitcher."

They both looked at the miniature of Miss Belle, resting on the oak desk. Blond curls framed an exceedingly pretty face. The large blue .eyes were heavily fringed in black lashes, and the smile was sweet.

"Not a clever girl like yourself, of course," Miss Munch admitted, "but a little lack of brains never stopped a man from falling in love."

Miss Halsey bit her lip and continued gazing at the picture. "No, and it doesn't stop the girl from falling in love with all the wrong gentlemen either. I fear there's some *tendre* growing between Belle and Basil."

"There's not a penny betwixt the pair of them," Miss Munch said. "Can't you just see our Belle living on a bone? She who has such a fondness for luxuries? What you've got to do is get her out where she'll be seen, and meet some richer *partis*, Miss Halsey. It's your bounden duty."

Miss Halsey sat on the edge of the bed, for there was no space in the room for a chair. "But how are we going to accomplish it, Munch? Aunt Hermione is not at all sociable. Here it is the end of May, the Season nearly over, and we haven't been to a single real party. Just a few poky little dos, you know, where Belle doesn't meet anyone."

"Don't you worry your head about that, Miss Halsey. There's many a twist in life. Just when everything seems impossible, that's when a new twist comes along and unravels all the rest."

Miss Halsey considered this ambiguous encouragement. It seemed to her that her life was pretty well unraveled already. Within the space of eighteen months she and Belle had lost their father and their home. Belle's Season had been nipped in the bud, she had very nearly been pressured into marrying an elderly neighbor, and was now encouraging the advances of a totally ineligible cousin. What was left to unravel?

With all Belle's beauty, surely she could attract the attention of some more suitable *parti* than Basil Pettigrew. The trouble was, Belle was one of those women made for marriage. Nothing else in life was of much interest to her. She would accept the first reputable offer that came along. And if Belle accepted Basil, what was to become of herself?

Miss Munch, satisfied that she had lifted her charge's spirits, went into the hall to seek assistance in moving the trunks, and Jane went to the mirror to tidy her hair. The image staring at her with somber eyes looked frustrated enough to strike someone. Jane admitted she did not take adversity well.

She disliked having to crowd herself and Belle in on Aunt Hermione. She hated being poor, and she was bored to flinders with the confined society of Catherine Street. If Belle married Basil, nothing would change. They would all four go on living here as they did at present. The answer must lie with herself. *She* must make a push to attach someone. At four and twenty, she was no longer quite a deb. It was time to give up girlish daydreams and face reality. She must seek an older gentleman, then, perhaps a widower, or some bachelor nabob hot from India, in a hurry to settle down and start his family.

She was still plenty young enough for that. Jane lifted the brush and drew it through her short curls, tousled from juggling the furnishings of her bedroom. Tints of peacock, gold, and purple reflected where the sunlight streamed on her raven hair. Her face was an oval of ivory, untouched as yet by time's passage so far as wrinkles or crow's-feet were concerned. Her eyes were two stormy pools of gray, deep and unfathomable as the ocean. Though her body was long and lean, it wasn't her figure that had kept her single. She might make a match yet if she could manage to control her tongue, and simper when a gentleman treated her as if she were a witless ninnyhammer, instead of a lady with a mind.

Before long, Belle Halsey came pelting up the stairs, her face aglow with excitement. Jane heard her and went to the door.

"What is it, Belle?" she asked.

"Cousin Basil has found a position!" Belle chirped. "Oh, isn't it exciting! You must come down at once and congratulate him, Jane."

Jane followed her sister down to the saloon, where Basil was outlining his good fortune to his mother. Jane was constantly surprised at how little he had changed over the years. She had first known him as a boy, visiting at Halsey Hall. A wispy, gangling, awkward child two years her junior, he had been firmly under her thumb. Now he stood six feet tall, still wispy and gangling and awkward, still not completely free of her thumb. The greatest change was a pair of spectacles added to conceal his rather nice brown eyes. Despite his unprepossessing appearance, Basil was likable.

Basil had some inclination toward the poetic style in his dress. His hair was worn a little longer than most, and allowed to fall wantonly over his forehead. His well-cut jacket of blue Bath cloth and fawn pantaloons were well enough, but on most occasions he was more likely to wear a neckerchief than a proper cravat. These tokens of the Muse were a strong attraction to Belle. Jane was happy to see them all set aside on this occasion, probably because he had been on an interview. He turned when the ladies entered the saloon. His glimmering spectacles immediately sought out Belle, who smiled softly at him. Only after they had exchanged one of their secret, speaking smiles did he turn to Jane.

"Congratulate me, cousin," he smiled. "You are looking at a wage earner."

Jane went forward and took his hand. "I couldn't be happier, Basil. Do tell us all about it."

He showed the ladies to the sofa and sat on a chair midway between it and his mother's seat. Mrs. Pettigrew was smiling in proud, maternal satisfaction. She had given up any pretense to beauty or fashion, and wore the raiments of a dowager. Her graying hair was concealed beneath a lace cap, and her dark gown was unadorned by anything except a mourning pin that held a lock of her late husband's hair. Yet the lineaments of her face pleased Jane, mirroring as they did some memory of her mother's mild expression and gray eyes.

"I've been hired by the British Museum," Basil announced. "I have old Beakey, a friend from Oxford, to thank for this. His uncle, Sir Lawrence Beaker, is in charge of a whole department."

His mother said, "How ideal for you, Basil. Your father always said it was not what you know, but whom you know. A foot in the door is the main thing. You must oil up to this Sir Lawrence Beaker, and you'll advance in your career. You will love working in a museum. All those artifacts and books and things."

"Yes, certainly I look forward to that, eventually."

The ladies exchanged a wary glance. "Does your job not begin at once, Basil?" his mother asked.

"I already have an office and a key, but not to the museum. For the nonce I will be looking after the Elgin Marbles at Burlington House. The government bought them from Lord Elgin, you must know, and they are to be packed up and sent off to the museum, but meanwhile I am their custodian."

"What are the Elgin Marbles, Basil?" Belle asked.

"Why, you must have read about them, Belle! The papers have been full of them. They are adornments, mostly from the Parthenon in Athens, which Lord Elgin retrieved and brought home safe to England. The whole place was blown to bits, for it was used as a powder magazine during some war, and that old Turk, Morosini, went at the statues and what not to carry them away. That was some time ago, however," he said vaguely.

Belle had heard of the Parthenon, but was a little unsteady as to exactly where, and what, it might be. Till she had time to study the matter, she spoke of other things. "And you will be guarding them at Burlington House. How lovely. May we see them?"

"Yes, certainly. You really ought to go and study them."

"May we see your office, too?" she asked. Where Basil spent his days was of more interest to her than marble statues.

His gentle smile revealed a complete understanding of her thoughts. "I have the carriage waiting. I hoped I might induce you to go this afternoon." He remembered Jane, and turned to her. "And you, too, Jane, if you like. And you, Mama . . ."

Mrs. Pettigrew declined the invitation, but was not loath to have the youngsters out of the house for a few hours, and encouraged the outing. In particular, she urged Jane to chaperon them. Not that she had anything against Belle Halsey, but there was no denying Basil could do better for himself than an undowered orphan with no expectations of future money.

Jane accepted eagerly. She had no intention of letting the two off together, but quite aside from that, she was keen to see the popular Elgin Marbles. She and Belle went for their bonnets and pelisses, and soon the trio was climbing into the carriage for the trip to Burlington House. Jane enjoyed the trot along the Strand and up Haymarket to Piccadilly. The roads were alive with fashionable carriages. Basil even nodded out the window to a few gentlemen, but did not pull the checkstring to stop and chat. She noticed with chagrin that masculine heads on the street strained for a glimpse of the pretty blonde by Basil's side. Surely Belle could nab one of them, if only she could get about a little.

Thus far, Belle was only mildly infatuated with Basil. She had been prey to many infatuations already. A more eligible *parti* could easily divert her attention, if only he showed up soon.

Burlington House was a huge, classical building with many portals. Basil led them to one of the lesser ones and through a tiled archway to his office. It was indeed an impressive sight after the cramped quarters of Catherine Street. Oak wainscoting climbed waist-high, and above it the plastered wall was hung with large old paintings, mainly landscapes by unrecognized artists.

"This is my desk," he said proudly. Belle smiled

with interest at the battered piece of lumber, which was large but serviceable.

"And you have a window," she pointed out. He also had a view of ten feet of grass, before another wall rose up to impede the vista.

"And bookcases. I can get my books out of the attic and bring them here," Basil said.

The simple speech reminded Jane most forcefully of how they had taken over his office at home. Basil's new office was complete with a threadbare carpet, drapes, and a few pieces of bric-a-brac. What it did not have, however, was more than two chairs.

"This is very handsome, Basil," Jane said. "Now shall we go and inspect the famous Marbles?"

"Yes, by Jove."

He led them along corridors to the exhibition room, where a goodly crowd was inspecting the artworks. Jane joined the throng, peering over shoulders and around heads to catch a glimpse of the shattered carvings. Her first glimpse was disappointing. She knew the carvings were ancient, but had not thought they would be in such poor repair. Hardly a single figure was intact. If the head was in place, the arms or legs were sure to be missing. She had to use her imagination to fill in the gaps, but certainly the works were beautiful. The frieze, in particular, a procession of the Athenian gods, was in fairly good repair.

While Jane studied it, an elegant young gentleman studied her, marveling that he had nearly refused his brother's request to come here. It was fate, of course, that had arranged the timing of their visit. The Fates loved him, and conspired to bring his wishes to fruition. He wore a smile of simple, pure refinement not unlike one of the Grecian statues.

An Attic smile, he would have called it himself, for Lord Romeo was an ardent lover of things Grecian. He had already named Miss Halsey *Athene*, till he could call her Lady Romeo, for of course he must marry her.

Chapter Two

*T*HE FATEFUL visit of Lord Romeo Rutledge to Burlington House was precipitated by a discussion between his mother, the Duchess of Stapford, and her elder son, the Marquess of Renfrew. Both were concerned about Lord Romeo's deepening state of melancholia, as they sat in the elegant gold saloon of Stapford House in Belgrave Square. No small part of the duchess's dismay was that she must *be* sitting in the great, pretentious, drafty chamber, and not comfortably home in Hampshire, tending her garden.

"I am truly concerned about the boy," she admitted to Renfrew. Concern lent a piqued tone to her words, and thrust a sharp stab of impatience through her bosom when she thought how she was missing the roses' best season at home. They would be climbing all over the trellises by now, and filling the air with their sweet scent.

The duchess, informally known as Stappy to her *intimes*, was not a beautiful lady. Her height would have qualified her for admission to the grenadiers, and her shoulders would not have disgraced the uniform either. Her face was designed on geometric lines: a perfectly square jaw, a straight wedge of nose, flat planes of cheeks. Her coiffure did nothing to soften this angular appearance. An indeterminate grayish-blond shade, it was dragged back into a knot. Renfrew always thought her eyes should be steel gray, but in fact they were an attractively deep shade of blue. Were it not for the slash of black eyebrows above them, one would be tempted to say they were feminine eyes.

The pattern card of elegance lounging in a *bergère* chair across from her was much prettier. It was one of nature's little jokes to have made the gentlemen of the house of Stapford exquisite beauties, and the ladies what was politely called plain. Lord Renfrew was of a height with his mama, approximately six feet. His mama envied his long-lashed blue eyes, his delicately chiseled face, and his lithe figure. What she did not envy, or even comprehend, try as she might, was that he could be bothered taking such pains with his toilette.

That blue jacket, for example, that clung to his lean body without so much as a crease, was the work of someone called Weston. Renfrew's tailor featured in his conversation with equal prominence to prime ministers or kings. She admired his flowered waistcoat enormously, but knew the pattern was too dainty for her. She would look absurd in rosebuds, much as she loved the live rose. Plain, dark colors were what her geometrical figure demanded.

"He'll get over it," Renfrew said in a languorous drawl. "He's been jilted before."

"Aye, but never by such a dasher as Lady Barbara Manfred. He had his heart set on marrying her, you must know, and now I read she is to have Lord Clivedon after all. It was very sudden, was it not?"

"The match had been brewing awhile," Renfrew replied. His mama nodded. Renfrew knew all the *on-dits*. "Lady Barbara wasn't right for Romeo, too hot at hand, and too rackety," he added, but with no air of censure.

"She was quite a scandal, which is why I thought her chaperon might let her marry Romeo—just to be rid of her. There is no denying Romeo is a little—odd. It is his sojourn in Greece that accounts for it, but his poor lungs—he could not tolerate England's climate. Fifteen years in the Mediterranean is enough to make anyone loony. Not that I mean to say Romeo is actually mad. Only different."

Renfrew listened with an air of amusement. "Romeo is delightfully mad, Mama," he said, again without censure. "There isn't another such interesting lunatic in all of England. He actually *thinks*. It is just that he doesn't bother thinking about practical things, like eating, and being civil to people, and coming in out of the rain. Given the proper wife, Romeo could handle life without being locked up, or shot—or hung. What we must do is find him a wife, and keeper, for I cannot like to see him leave us again."

The duchess clicked her tongue against her teeth. "He'd not settle for some harridan, Renfrew. Romeo is very nice in his requirements. Lady Barbara is a stunner, for all her shabby behavior."

"He'd settle for an ax murderess, if she had the right face, which is to say, a classical face. Not that we shall hobble him with a murderess. Just some strong-willed, practical lady of good common sense."

His mother turned a derisive eye on her son. "To say the words with no bark on 'em, what sensible gel would have him? He'd make a laughingstock of her with his antics. He's insulted every worthy in London, by calling names. As to keeping an appointment, if he happened to see a lintel or column that caught his fancy, he'd stay mooning over it for a fortnight and forget to visit his lady, for you know he never can draw himself away from anything Grecian. No, Renfrew, I think we must let him return to Athens. He speaks of doing so, and I come to think it is the proper place for him."

"His lungs are cured now, Mama," Renfrew pointed out. "Why consign the lad to Greece? The lady who marries him need not be well-dowered. Penniless ladies are not so nice in their requirements. A genteel lady with her pockets to let would be inclined to overlook the odd missed appointment. Indeed, she would appreciate it. And Romeo is biddable enough when he is in love."

That Renfrew condescended to discuss the matter told his mother it was important to him, more important than his bored demeanor would suggest. "Do you have someone in mind?" she asked hopefully.

"Till now, I hadn't bent my mind to the question. We thought Romeo would marry Lady Barbara, but as that is over, I shall review the ladies of my acquaintance and find him a wife. She can take him off to his Hampshire estate and let him build Grecian temples. That'll keep him happy and out of mischief, and close enough that we may continue seeing him. I like Romeo." He sounded surprised at the admission.

The mischief referred to, though Lord Renfrew did not wish to trouble his mother with the tale, was the daughter of a certain publican in Taunton. Romeo had begun by planning an affair with the female. Her father had objected, at which point Romeo had fallen in love with Lady Barbara Manfred instead. When she accepted an offer from Lord Clivedon, Romeo began to talk up the idea of marrying the woman from Taunton. Marriage with such a person was out of the question, but if marriage was what he had in mind, let him marry a decent woman.

A shadow in the hallway beyond caught Renfrew's attention, and he looked up to see his brother hovering there. The words from a poem came to mind: "alone and palely loitering." That was how Romeo was behaving lately, and it pierced Renfrew with sorrow to see it. It was obviously his duty to rectify the matter.

He detached himself gracefully from the chair and went to meet Romeo. "So there you are! We were just speaking of you," he said heartily.

"No ill, I hope?" Romeo inquired. He wore a detached, remote smile of ineffable sweetness. Lord Romeo was slight of stature, but his appearance was something quite out of the ordinary. His beautiful locks were bleached nearly white, and arranged *à la cherubim*. His eyes, a clear, celestial blue, glowed with an inner light, and had even longer lashes than Lord Renfrew's. He was a very tulip of fashion, but in the poetic style. At his throat he wore a silk kerchief of cerulean blue, tied in the Belcher fashion.

"Certainly not," his brother assured him.

"Then it must have been a short conversation," Romeo sighed. "What good is to be said of me? What have I, with all my talents, accomplished? A few paintings, a few verses, of which not more than a dozen lines will be immortal. Was I put on earth for so little cause? I am become an albatross around the family's neck. I shall not trouble you much longer, James. This albatross is about to slip into the sea, like that of the ancient mariner."

Renfrew felt a spasm of alarm, as he gazed at his forlorn brother. Worry lent a sharp edge to his words. "Don't talk nonsense!"

"Ah, James, I hear the very echo of Papa in that brusque speech. You scowl and snarl because you are sorry for me, and have the English dislike of tender emotions. But you misunderstand my meaning, brother. I am not speaking of drowning myself. Perhaps one day, but not yet. I have definitely decided to return to Greece. England is not fit for human beings. It should be given back to the wolves."

Renfrew's heart stopped pounding. "But you just got here! And London . . ."

Romeo held out a white, long-fingered hand. "Pray do not cite Dr. Johnson's tedious epithet that when a man is tired of London, he is tired of life. When a man is tired of London, he is ready for life, but he will not find it here, amid the fog and ugly buildings and noisy chatter of barbarians. The islands send out their siren call, and I shall heed it. I have lingered too long in this limbo. I found myself anticipating a bite of roast beef in the kitchen just now. Imagine to what depths I have sunk! To even *consider* eating an innocent fellow animal. I particularly admire the placidity of bovines, too."

Though it was a relief to realize suicide was not in Romeo's mind, Renfrew was grieved to hear his brother planned to leave England. He sought for something to distract Romeo. Bright, golden sunlight streamed through the windows. It was the end of May, and outside Romeo might find the weather enjoyable.

"Well, you shan't be leaving today. Before you go, let us take your carriage out for a ride," Renfrew suggested.

"It is kind of you to try to distract me, James. I really do appreciate it, but there is nowhere to go in London," Romeo said simply.

"Take him to a park, Renfrew," the duchess said.

Romeo cast a sorry eye on her. "Why do you speak as though I were not here, or a helpless old man, Mama? Just so did you used to speak of Grandfather Stapford, before he died, but he was deaf. I hear perfectly, and I do not wish to go to a park. I want to go home. My psyche is pining for Athens."

James had the inspiration of the Elgin Marbles, tokens from Athens, and suggested viewing them.

"I am opposed on principle to paying to see them," Romeo said firmly. "It is tantamount to approving of Lord Elgin's rape of the Parthenon."

"You mean you haven't seen them yet?" Renfrew asked, shocked.

"Certainly I have. I saw them at the Acropolis before Elgin had them removed. They were in a shambles, half of them scattered on the ground. The works of Phidias, imagine! A sacrilege. I sketched the head of one particularly fine piece—one of the graces. It had become severed from the body. I wonder if Elgin brought it to London."

"Why don't we go and see?" Renfrew tempted.

Romeo remembered that hauntingly beautiful head, with a gentle smile. He thought it must be Thalia, goddess of bloom, for she appeared to be blooming with rapture. "You didn't notice if Thalia was there?" Romeo asked, with an air of curiosity.

"Thalia who?" Renfrew was so unwise as to ask.

"Ah, James, even you are as ignorant as a swan. What do they teach you at Oxford? Thalia is one of the three goddesses of fertility. I cannot like to satisfy Elgin by paying him for his depredations, but I see I must accompany you to view the Marbles, for you have not appreciated them as you ought. Come, we shall go now. Pray say good-bye to Mama for me. I mean to show her how it feels to be spoken of as though one were absent."

Renfrew bit back a rueful smile and turned to his mother. "We're off, Mama." He winked broadly over Romeo's shoulder, and went after his curled beaver and malacca cane. Renfrew pointed out some of the more appetizing sights of London as the carriage hastened toward Burlington House. Lord Romeo closed his eyes and shuddered in revulsion.

"Tell me when we arrive. You know I become ill at the sight of English architecture. The vulgarity of domes, in particular, quite unmans me. I hold Wren responsible in large part for this blight that London has become."

As the Earl of Burlington had had his mansion built in the classical style, Romeo was able to open his eyes as he entered. At the doorway, he took up a catalog of the Marbles, and calmly told the man at the door, "I shall not be paying, but lest you think me merely clutch-fisted, I want you to know I shall be giving a large donation to my favorite charity."

On this speech he swept past the doorman. Renfrew handed the man fare for them both, and the incident passed without fuss. Lord Romeo was sufficiently known in London that people stared when he entered the room. The crowd parted before him, as though he were a monarch, and soon he stood in front of the shattered marbles, shaking his head. People listened to hear his pronouncement.

"The Three Fates," he murmured. "Was there ever anything so exquisite? I feel the hand of the master in the drape of that gown. Phidias, of course. No underling was responsible for *that* drape, though I discern the clumsier hand of Ictinus, the architect, in some of these carvings. See the columnlike arm he has put on the third Fate."

Renny looked at the headless ladies and said, "A pity the heads didn't make it."

"*Ex pede, Herculem.* Pythagoras deduced Hercules' stature from length of his foot, and from the sublime toes of this Fate, I can appreciate the genius of Phidias."

Romeo fell into one of his trances, and after a moment, his brother gently nudged his elbow. "Shall we move along and see the Birth of Athene?"

"You go, James. I shall stay and communicate a moment with the shade of Phidias. I can see at a glance that Elgin's foragings are largely rubble. It quite crushes me to see these relics from the age of Pericles come to such a fate. The metopes are practically dust."

"The frieze is in fair repair."

"James! One does not visit an art gallery to admire the *frames*. But perhaps I shall find Thalia."

Renfrew finally got his brother moved along, to permit the other viewers to see the Fates. While Romeo assessed some portions of the frieze, Renfrew glanced around at the crowd, wondering if he might see a friend to pass the next half hour with, or perhaps a pretty lady to pique Romeo's interest. E'er long, his practiced eye had discovered a diamond of the first water.

Golden curls nestled around a pretty little face.

He saw Belle Halsey in profile first, and admired the slight tilt of her nose. By edging closer, he got a look at her from the front, for he knew Romeo would not be tempted by a gap tooth, or a squinty eye, and a profile might be concealing such faults. The young lady was a very pineapple of perfection. Her eyes were wide and dewy, her lips a rosebud, and her expression of a sweetness to challenge Romeo's. Who could she be? It was strange such a beauty had not come to his attention before now.

Renfrew took a quick look at her partner, and thought he had seen the man before, possibly at Oxford. Not his own year, but surely he knew that thin-faced scholar with spectacles. He would speak to the man, and scrape an acquaintance if he didn't know him already.

Lord Romeo eventually parted company with Phidias and looked around for his brother. Across the room, he beheld perfection. The breath caught in his lungs, and he murmured "Pallas Athene," in an awed whisper. However, it was not the softness and grace of Belle Halsey that filled his ideals of perfection. The other lady had the air of firmness and composure of Zeus' own daughter. Her high, clear brow bespoke wisdom, and a certain firmness of mouth and jaw suggested her powers in combat. But for a spear and shield, and of course some anachronism in toilette—easily remedied—she was the very incarnation of Pallas Athene.

Lord Romeo wafted forward on winged feet till he stood within touching distance of his new ideal. He didn't speak, but he stared with such awful intensity that Miss Halsey's sixth sense sent a shiver up her spine. She turned and found herself gazing at a rather small Adonis. Smiling and simpering at wayward gentlemen was not her way. Her nostrils dilated in annoyance, and she said rather curtly, "May I help you, sir?"

She couldn't have reacted in a manner to please him more unless she had pulled a spear out of her reticule and attacked him. Her haughty stare was the proper reaction for a modern-day Athene. As she watched, his soft lips lifted in a vague smile, and his blue eyes seemed lit from behind. "Yes, you may save my life, if you will be so kind," he said gently.

Miss Halsey blinked in surprise. "Are you ill, sir?" she asked.

"I was close to expiring, but you have made me well. Allow me to present myself. I am Romeo, a loyal subject of your Athens."

At this peculiar speech, Miss Halsey looked around for Basil, as it was clear she had run into a lunatic. Basil and Belle had wandered along to admire the frieze. "You are mistaken, sir. I do not come from Athens," she said sharply, and turned to leave.

Romeo followed at her heels. "To deny it is to say apples do not come from trees, or milk from cows."

"I come from West Sussex, sir—not that it is any of your concern."

"Ah! I have heard of Sussex."

Miss Halsey stopped in her tracks. The man was a foreigner, then. That explained, to some extent, his odd behavior. His appearance was more than respectable, and his manner so extremely mild and courteous that she decided to turn him off politely. "You speak English very well," she said. "Where are you from?"

"I have already told you, indirectly. I am from Athens."

"Athens? Then the Marbles are of considerable interest to you, no doubt."

"I cherish every crumb, for they brought us together—at last."

That odd feeling that the man had escaped from Bedlam came washing over Jane again, and she began to edge away. "Well, I hope you enjoy them."

Romeo smiled more broadly. "You shall not escape, Athene. I have many swift arrows in my quiver." He shimmered after her, moving smoothly, as though on skates. Jane found her companions and ran the last few yards to join them.

Chapter Three

"*B*ASIL, HELP me!" she exclaimed. "A lunatic has been pestering me. He thinks I'm from Athens." As she spoke, she looked fearfully over her shoulder. The vision was drawing nearer. "That's the man," she said. "Can you get rid of him?"

In the confusion, Jane had not realized the man standing beside Basil was actually with him. Till he spoke to Basil, she took him for another viewer of the artworks.

Renfrew clenched his jaw in chagrin. How very like Romeo to have spoked his own wheel. A few moments conversation with Basil Pettigrew had informed him of the Incognita's name, and that she was a "Miss." Any cousin of Pettigrew's was bound to be of that genteel but not wealthy class that might welcome an alliance with a noble house. Miss Belle's beauty was great enough that Romeo would admire her.

"Allow me to present my brother, Lord Romeo,"

Renfrew said. As Romeo joined the party, he cast a triumphant glance at his prey.

"A great ox stands on my tongue," Romeo said with a bow to Miss Halsey. "I should be apologizing for my former incoherence, but it might offend the gods, who proffered the gift of our acquaintance. I'm sorry, I didn't catch your name."

Basil frowned at Romeo, but as it dawned on him that he was Lord Renfrew's brother, he bowed and presented the ladies. Renfrew looked expectantly, waiting for Romeo to discover Miss Belle. That he had developed a fleeting passion for the older lady was no surprise. Romeo was in and out of love the way other men were in and out of their jackets. Once he noticed the superior charms of the younger filly, he'd surely succumb to her.

Miss Belle received no more than a cursory nod, and before you could shake a stick, Romeo was making a sublime ass of himself. He turned a fatuous smile on Renfrew. "I shall never forget your insisting we come here, James. The gods were working through you on this occasion. To think, I might never have met Miss Halsey."

He could no longer keep his eyes from Jane. His head turned inexorably to her and he said, "I wish to make you my firm friend for all eternity. As a scholar of Greek, I know we secure our friends not by asking favors, but by granting them. I shall honor you with a tour of these artworks."

"I was just doing that myself," Basil mentioned.

Romeo examined him curiously. "Let each man exercise the art he knows. You cannot teach a crab to walk straight, and you cannot teach an Englishman to appreciate the sublimity of Phidias."

"Then there's no point in your endeavoring to teach me," Jane said. "I, too, am English."

"You soar above mere nationality. *You* are eternal woman," Romeo replied, and took her elbow to lead her away.

She shook him off rather abruptly and directed a demanding eye on his brother. It was at this point that Jane first took any real notice of the brother, and a glance was enough to awaken her to the charms lurking there. Renfrew stood, undecided. It seemed Romeo had already made his choice. In this mood, there was no point trying to dissuade him. Miss Halsey would do as well as her sister—perhaps better. She was certainly a strong-willed young lady, and Romeo would require a firm keeper.

"Let us all go," Renfrew said, and joined Miss Halsey on her other side.

Jane felt trapped, and resented being coerced to look at the artworks again. She stopped short and said, "Actually I've seen the Marbles already. I believe my party is about to leave now, if you will excuse me."

Romeo turned a helpless eye to his brother. "Stop her, James," he said. "Or at least discover where she dwells, that I may go to her."

"I can but try to persuade her." As Renfrew placed a proprietary hand on Jane's elbow, he gave his most charming smile. Jane found herself gazing into a pair of deep blue eyes. Her gaze flickered over the rest of Renfrew. Everything about the man was of the first stare, from his stylish Brutus hairdo to his exquisitely-tailored jacket and intricately tied cravat. The hand on her elbow was adorned with an emerald, set in gold. He was exactly the kind of man she dreamed of, and as Romeo showed no sign of accompanying them, she allowed herself to be led back to the Marbles.

"My brother speaks without thinking sometimes." Renfrew smiled in a conspiratorial way. "I apologize for his manners, but I must say I admire his taste."

Jane felt a smile bloom spontaneously at his speech, and the rather intimate manner he had adopted. "Oh, yes, the Marbles are exquisite," she said breathlessly.

Renfrew gave a flirtatious laugh. "Are we discussing the Marbles, Miss Halsey?"

She tossed her head pertly. "*I* am," she replied.

He examined her closely. "The Marbles are fine enough, but you must own they lack liveliness." It occurred to Renfrew there might be a second gentleman in the Halseys' party, and he glanced around. "Are there just the three of you?" he asked.

"Yes, my sister and I came with our cousin."

"I feared there might be a beau—a fiancé—lurking in the wings," he said, and listened sharply for her answer. What he sought for Romeo was an unattached lady, who might be snapped up quickly.

"I have no fiancé." Jane saw the gleam of satisfaction light his eye, and could only stare in disbelief.

"Lady Luck smiles on me today. Do you believe in luck, Miss Halsey?"

"Yes, indeed. I have encountered both sides of that capricious damsel."

He looked interested. "Indeed? I look forward to hearing an explanation of that remark." It sounded like the loss of either a beau or a fortune. Either would serve his ends equally well.

"That's a long story." It was a tale she had no intention of bringing forth, and she immediately changed the subject. "Your brother has just returned from Greece, I understand."

"Yes, he was raised there, for reasons of health. He's perfectly cured now," he added hastily.

"Then he'll be remaining in England?"

"It is the hope of the family that he will. We feel that if he married an Englishwoman, he might settle in comfortably."

Renfrew regarded Jane from the corner of his eye as he spoke. He detected no particular interest, but no aversion either.

"I suggest a less aggressive attack, if he approaches other ladies as he did me," she suggested.

Unaware of the precise nature of Romeo's attack on Miss Halsey, Renfrew replied, "Oh, there is something to be said for a direct approach, don't you think? We Stapfords don't tarry when we find what we want."

They strolled around for a few moments till they met the rest of the party coming the other way.

"Did you have any luck?" Romeo demanded eagerly of his brother. "What is her address?"

Renfrew gave him a quelling look and said, "Why don't we all go somewhere for coffee, and become better acquainted? Are you free, Mr. Pettigrew?"

"It is practically closing time. I daresay it would be all right." No one was likely to complain if he stepped out with the sons of a famous duke, and Basil was fully alive to the benefit to be derived from noble patrons.

"My brother, Lord Romeo, will tell us about Greece," Renfrew said, and went on talking to distract the group as he led them out. "He is an ardent Grecophile, if there is any such word."

Romeo, seeing that some further inducements were needed to win the lady, said, "I am very wealthy. My father is a duke."

Jane stared at such a blunt exhibition of his

status, and could not think of any sane reply. "That's nice," she said.

Renfrew glared, and Romeo fell silent. He followed, sensing it was for James to mend the rift. James was an excellent brother. His heart swelled with gratitude.

Miss Halsey's mind was all in a whirl at the day's unusual activities. Romeo she considered a confirmed bedlamite, but she was not immune to the superior charms of his brother. In Lord Renfrew the beauty of the younger brother was all there, magnified and purged of the imperfections.

He was completely rational, which was the first blessing. He was better formed, with broad shoulders and a lean, athletic body. On his mobile face she read breeding and intelligence, unmarred by any mania for Greece. In short, he was the kind of gentleman she had been hoping to meet, and she soon responded warmly to his conversation.

"So you are Pettigrew's cousin," Renfrew said. "We were at Oxford together a few years ago. The acquaintance slipped. It was pleasant to meet him again. We must get together soon and show you young ladies around town. Are you remaining long in London?"

"We are living here now, with our Aunt Pettigrew."

Renfrew turned a brightly questioning eye on her. "Your sister, perhaps, is not out, but how does it come I haven't seen *you* at any of the dos, Miss Halsey?"

"We live in a small way," she said, disliking to admit it.

Romeo nudged his brother's elbow and said in his fluting and perfectly audible whisper, "When they admit it so freely, it shows good breeding at least."

Jane's next speech was designed to inform him they were not quite nobody. "Actually I was presented a few years ago, and my sister a little later, but her Season was cut short by my father's illness and death."

"You are an orphan?" Romeo inquired eagerly. "Excellent, James," he hissed. "I shan't have to confront her papa. That is the worst part of offering for a lady. I shan't mind speaking to the cousin."

Renfrew did his mental arithmetic and accurately gauged Jane's age as "a little past the prime," which was all to the good. She wouldn't be besieged by offers. Before they all met at the carriages, Renfrew had an inkling of the Halseys' background. Such details as dowry (if any) and precise lineage could be discovered later. They were thoroughly respectable ladies fallen on hard times. It could hardly be better. Miss Halsey seemed sensible; she would soon come to realize the advantages of a match with Romeo: wealth, position, a life of ease. She'd snatch at the offer, once she realized Romeo was harmless.

The destination was chosen, a coffee shop on the Strand, and the ladies both went with Basil to meet the gentlemen there. "That was a bit of a shocker, what?" Basil said. "Lord Renfrew greeted me like a long-lost brother, and he never had a word to say to me at Oxford. It is my position at the British Museum that impressed him. He mentioned he has an uncle on the Board of Directors."

"A marquess, Jane!" Belle smiled. "Basil says he is a marquess, imagine. And he seemed very taken with you."

"Wouldn't I vault up the ladder with the Duke of Stapford for a sponsor!" Basil smiled.

"Lord Romeo gave me quit a turn," Jane replied,

but pleasantly. A marquess could be forgiven a dotty brother.

"I thought he was sweet," Belle said. "A little odd, to be sure, the way he didn't look at anyone but you. My nose is quite out of joint."

Basil cleared his throat nervously and said, "What shall we say if Renfrew wants to call, Jane? Will you encourage him?"

"I see no reason to discourage him," she said contentedly.

"The Stapfords are the tip of the *ton*, you must know. I don't see how Mama can entertain a marquess."

Belle gurgled. "Goose! It's not Aunt Hermione who will have to entertain him. He'll take Jane out—to balls and routs and drives. It sounds lovely."

"It sounds a trifle fast to me," Basil worried, "though too good a connection to let slip through our fingers if his intentions are honorable." It would be for Mama to decide.

Renfrew had already arranged a table when they entered the coffee shop. Romeo wafted forward to draw Jane's chair beside his own, but as Renfrew was on her other side, she didn't object. They ordered coffee and cakes, and settled in to further the acquaintance.

"Do you ride?" Renfrew asked Jane.

"I adore it, but we—we didn't bring our mounts to London," she said. The acquaintance was too new to give details of her Uncle Horace's nip-cheese ways.

Romeo liked riding, and his brother said, "That's no problem. I can find you a mount. We'll arrange it soon. Does your sister ride as well?"

"She loves it." Jane smiled. How fortunate they'd brought their habits with them.

"Excellent, we'll make up a party soon." He looked a question at Basil: Pettigrew could accompany Miss Belle, and Romeo could escort Miss Halsey, leaving himself well out of it.

"Unfortunately my cousin won't be able to come with us," Jane said. "He has just taken a position with the British Museum."

"Of course. Then it will be just we four," Renfrew said, resigning himself to the inevitable. He examined Belle a moment, and found her not without charm, though country girls were not his favorite sort. He preferred more sophisticated ladies. "I expect you also dance?" he asked Jane.

"Now that we are out of mourning, we can dance again. It's a pity the Season is nearly over."

Renfrew batted his hand carelessly. "There are plenty of routs and smaller parties all summer. Finding a venue will be no problem. There's always Stapford House," he added as an afterthought.

"That's my family's house, in Belgrave Square," Romeo added. "It is said to be one of the finest in London, if you can call Palladian architecture fine."

Jane and Belle exchanged a glance of surprised delight. The future shone brightly indeed, with promises of rides and drives and parties. Lord Romeo was a small price to pay for this bonanza. Jane turned a forgiving face to him.

"You're very quiet, Lord Romeo," she said.

In her dulcet tones he heard the myriad laughter of the ocean waves. "Silence is often the wisest thing," he replied enigmatically.

"Are you thinking some deep, Grecian thoughts?"

"You read me like a book. I am thinking of home. Soon I shall be there."

Jane was very happy to hear it. "You're leaving

England, then, are you?" She looked a question at Renfrew, who had mentioned his brother's marrying and settling in the country.

"We could not be happy here," Romeo answered.

"I am perfectly happy here.'

'The Phidias collection brought home most forcefully that I am living in the wrong country. I must go home—but can I leave Phidias behind? There's the question."

"There must be plenty of other works by him in Greece," Jane said.

"Yes, but there is only one Parthenon, the most remarkable structure in the world. Western culture culminated in Greece, Grecian culture in Athens, Athens in the Acropolis, and the Acropolis in the Parthenon. And to arrive and see it now, standing like a ruined hag, destroyed less by the tooth of time and earthquake and war than by man . . . well, one really ought to do what one can to restore it. I think I must take the Marbles back with me."

Jane blinked in astonishment, and turned to Lord Renfrew. "The price paid was thirty-five thousand pounds, Romeo," his brother told him dampingly.

"If I sold my Hampshire property . . ."

"The government would never sell them," Basil said. Now that he was working for the museum, he felt he could speak ex cathedra on such matters.

"The government would sell its soul for money," Romeo answered calmly. "I daresay they'd expect to make a profit. They'd take fifty thousand. I cannot be the only man in England with a conscience. I shall set up a subscription. Will you help me, Miss Halsey?"

"I'm afraid not. Greece is still at war. Why let more invaders destroy the Marbles? They're safer here."

"Till Bonaparte escapes again," Romeo said. "Athene should display more wisdom, and more love for her city. You, who had the wisdom to win Athens with your gift of the olive tree, wresting it from Poseidon, who gave only a horse, must not desert it in its hour of need. I shall restore the Parthenon in your honor."

"You do me too much honor," she assured him.

"Never enough." Romeo turned to his brother, but spoke in a perfectly audible voice. "May we go home now, James? I cannot make any headway with Miss Halsey in front of so many people. I shall call on her tomorrow, and try to wrest her away from the others."

Renfrew leveled a quelling stare at Romeo. "Perhaps it is time to be going. It was a great delight to meet you, Miss Halsey. May I do myself the honor of calling on you soon, to settle plans for future outings?"

"I look forward to it."

"Don't forget to get her address," Romeo urged.

Renfrew's smile was tinged with embarrassment. "You heard my command," he said softly to Jane. "I require an address."

She gave it, not without a sense of apprehension. What would Renfrew think of her residing on Catherine Street? He nodded, perfectly unfazed by the modest street.

The party took their leave and went to their separate carriages. Renfrew damped down his temper and said to his brother, "It would be wiser if you didn't harp so on Greece to Miss Halsey. She was just beginning to warm up to you."

"It is kind of you to fret for me, James, but I can manage it. I have two gods to help me: Persuasion and Compulsion."

"Yes, the persuasion of your title and fortune, and any compulsion Miss Halsey's unfortunate condition might induce in her. You pushed the family glory a little too strong, my friend."

"I shall forgive you those slurs on my beloved. As if Athene would be swayed by titles and money. I said it for her cousin's benefit. He will run home with a report of me. It is tyranny's disease, to trust no friend, and you *are* my friend, I hope. But I must trust in my own discretion."

"You do that, Romeo. *Try* if you can display some discretion."

Renfrew saw that his words fell on deaf ears. Romeo leaned his head against the squabs of the carriage and fell into a reverie. He seemed to be murmuring some Greek poem, but at least he had ceased speaking of hopping the next ship to Greece.

Chapter Four

"*I* TOLD you so! Didn't I tell you so?" Miss Munch exclaimed, when she heard the delightful news. "And a marquess to boot. Lord, was there ever such luck. And your uncle raping young Missie over the coals for not marrying that old Rankin. Your sister will find you a lord, too, Missie, once she is a marquisite."

"He is only coming to call, Munch," Jane told her, but she was too happy to castigate her faithful servant.

"I'll dart up to the attics and bring down your riding habits and ball gowns for pressing. Where we shall keep them I'm sure *I* don't know." Munch flew up to the attic that moment and began hauling down the gowns and riding habits.

The sisters were so thrilled with Jane's conquest, they wouldn't have cared if the gowns were kept in the saloon. Mrs. Pettigrew, not blind to the possibilities of the connection with the Duke of Stapford's son, did better than that: the gowns were kept in her own room, where her closets were pretty much to let.

"A pity Basil will not be a part of these expeditions you mention, Jane," she said, "but you will remember to put his name forward. He is a little backward. Imagine his not telling me he knew Lord Renfrew. I'm sure I read Renfrew's name in the journals every second day. Basil does not realize what an impression he makes on people. I daresay there are a dozen such influential gentlemen he might have spoken to, and done better for himself than sitting in a dusty museum all day, guarding statues."

Over the next few days, a great air of excitement invaded the modest house on Catherine Street. Lord Renfrew and Lord Romeo came daily to take the ladies for rides in the park, drives into the country, and to view an art exhibit at Somerset House. It was during this last outing that Renfrew found a few minutes to do some gentle quizzing regarding Miss Halsey's circumstances, and give her a hint of how marriage to Romeo might enhance them. He approached the topic by careful indirection.

"It's a pity Pettigrew couldn't enjoy these outings with us," he said.

"Yes, but he takes his work very seriously. He is a hard worker." With her aunt's injunction in mind, Jane added, "His education really ought to merit a better position than he has at the moment."

"No doubt he will advance quickly, if he is both clever and a worker," Renfrew replied. "I hope he doesn't take it amiss that we are entertaining Miss Belle for him. Or am I mistaken in thinking there is an understanding between them?"

Jane frowned. "Oh, no! Not an understanding. Belle is young; she has often fancied herself in love before. I am rather hoping she will meet someone more eligible, for it happens that Belle has no dowry. I received my mother's portion."

Renfrew listened closely. His plan would advance more smoothly if it were Miss Halsey who had no dowry. He disliked to ask vulgar questions, but suggested, "Perhaps you could share with her."

"I shall, if it is necessary, though ten thousand split two ways is not much of a dowry for either of us." She gave a fleeting look at Renfrew as she spoke. It was the first time anything as important as dowries had come up between them. It almost sounded as if he were thinking of marriage.

Renfrew looked across the crowded room to Romeo, and said, "If you marry a gentleman of substance, the size of the dowry won't matter, will it?"

Following his gaze, Jane thought he was looking at Belle. She felt a queer fluttering in her breast. Two spots of color splotched her cheeks, and when she spoke, her voice was unsteady. "No, it would not matter much."

Renfrew smiled softly. The beam from his deep blue eyes bathed her in happy confusion. Then he put a proprietary hand on her elbow and said, "Shall we rejoin the others?"

Romeo had taken up a position in front of Gainsborough's much admired painting of Mr. and Mrs. Robert Andrews.

"I daresay the Andrewses could sue," he said, tilting his head to the side, the better to criticize the work. "Surely they could not *both* be so ugly, and so much in the same style, with those awful wall eyes, and Flemish noses."

The ladies had become accustomed to Romeo's outrageous utterances by this time.

"The little dog is sweet," Belle said.

"The dog is in profile," Romeo pointed out. "If Gainsborough had tackled him head-on, he, too, would be walleyed. Let us see some other pictures. This one is making me quite ill." He turned and took Jane's hand. "I shall overcome nausea by basking in the glow of Pallas Athene," he said, and led her off to view less revolting pictures.

Jane cast a conspiratorial smile at Renfrew over her shoulder. It was one of the less pleasant features of their outings that she so often fell prey to Romeo's infatuation. As Renfrew took it in good part, she did likewise, but sometimes she wished Renfrew would intervene.

The Countess Lieven spotted Romeo and darted across the room to see what new outrage she could pick up to scandalize society. "You have come to poke fun at our artists, eh, Lord Romeo?" she prodded archly.

"The trip was quite unnecessary," Lord Romeo replied. "Gainsborough needs no assistance from me to reveal his total lack of talent."

"Did you see Lawrence's portrait of Lady Cowper?" she asked, hoping for some disparagement of her dear friend and sister patroness of Almack's.

"Yes, it is an astonishing feat of legerdemain. He has painted a portrait that actually resembles Lady Cowper, yet makes her look pretty. You really ought to sit for him, Countess Lieven. He might even be able to do something with you."

Renfrew hastened forward to prevent disaster, and overheard the last of his brother's remark. "He would be a poor artist indeed if he could not make Countess Lieven look pretty," Renfrew said, with an apologetic smile.

Romeo examined the lady at length, with a curiously impersonal gaze. His eye traveled from hair to eyes to nose and back again. No spark of admiration animated his examination. "I have always admired the countess's ears," he decided, then added with a mischievous smile, "I understand they are the sharpest pair in London."

The countess's lips thinned in annoyance. "You are thinking of my tongue, Lord Romeo," she replied. "You have not introduced me to your friends," she added, turning her attention to the young ladies.

"The Misses Halsey, from West Sussex. It's somewhere in England," he said. Romeo turned to Jane. "I didn't think you would be interested to meet Countess Lieven. People only court her for tickets to Almack's, and you would not enjoy that stuffy court."

Countess Lieven took all his insults as prime jokes, and ran around the room to repeat them, before someone beat her to it. She also announced to the other patronesses that the Misses Halsey were not quite the sort of young ladies they were interested in.

All details of the outings were dutifully reported back at Catherine Street. "The Countess Lieven!" Mrs. Pettigrew exclaimed. "My dear, you will receive vouchers to Almacks, certainly. Basil would meet everyone there. Even the Prince attends. He is a bosom bow of Lieven."

Belle remained below talking to her aunt when Jane went upstairs to report to Miss Munch. "I was just wondering while you were gone," Miss Munch said, "if there is any hope of Missie attaching the young brother. That would really break the icing on the cake if you could both nab lords. It would please your aunt no end. She grinned like a Cheshire cat when I mentioned it."

"I wish it would happen, but I see no sign of it. It would give me a few moments in private with Renfrew if Belle could attach his brother. But then I don't suppose Belle would care for Romeo."

"She never has a word to say against him. She thinks him quite a Donis, whatever that is. Does Lord Renfrew never find a chance to cuddle you at all?" Munch asked.

"Courting is more formal in London than at home," Jane replied. That must account for any little reticence on Renfrew's part. He was obviously smitten, or why did he dance attendance on her?

When it occurred to Renfrew that a broader field of acquaintances was necessary to bring forth the desired social invitations for the entertainment of the ladies, he arranged a theater party. The Halseys were introduced to as many of his friends as possible. The outing brought forth cards to two unexceptionable rout parties. At a gentle hint from Jane, Renfrew arranged for Basil Pettigrew to receive cards as well. He was happy to do it, as it relieved him somewhat from squiring Belle, though he meant to tag along to smooth Romeo's thorny path.

On the evening of the first rout at Lady Sifton's, the Halseys took special pains with their toilettes. Jane chose a rose Italian crepe gown, ruched with lace and bows around the hem. The gown set off her ivory complexion and raven hair, and excitement put a sparkle in her eyes.

"Our first real London party, Belle." She smiled. "And how lovely you look. You will attract the attention of some gentleman worthy of you," she prophesied.

Belle smiled at her reflection. As she was no longer technically a deb, she had ventured to leave off white and wore a powder blue gown, the under-skirt spangled with silver sequins. "Basil always says I look fine in this gown." She smiled.

Miss Munch thought the sisters, one so stately and dark of complexion, the other a gentle blonde, would cause quite a stir. "Like night and day," she said, shaking her head fondly at them. "It's hard to say who is prettier. There won't be a lady at the party to touch either of you. They must all be mad as wet dogs at the competition you've brought them."

The party did receive its fair share of attention when they entered the crowded room. Basil gained Belle's hand for the first dance, which left Jane with two partners. She smiled an apology at Romeo.

"There are several young ladies waiting for partners," she pointed out.

Romeo glanced along the wall uninterestedly. "You must not worry about James. He is a famous flirt."

On this speech he took Jane's hand to lead her away. Accustomed to his strange and arbitrary ways, she thought little of it. She cast a helpless, laughing look at James. "The next dance, Renfrew?" she asked.

Renfrew, very well pleased with the outcome, bowed and said, "I look forward to it, Miss Halsey." He made his choice of the available ladies and seemed content with his partner. It wasn't till he stood up with Jane that he began to perceive her confusion.

"Your brother is impossible," she said with a re-signed *tsk*. "You move too slowly, sir. I must say, you did not try very hard for the first dance with me," she added with a coquettish smile.

Renfrew's quick frown of puzzlement passed unnoticed by Jane, but her speech gave him pause. Was it possible Miss Halsey was implying she favored himself? He was stunned at the possibility, but as he reviewed their past meetings, it occurred to him that the mistake might easily have come about. He was always at Romeo's elbow, trying to prevent an innocent outing from degenerating into chaos. He enjoyed Miss Halsey's company, and made no effort to conceal it. Flirtation was his natural mode of conduct with a young lady. He could hardly conceive of any other, but he must be much more discreet in future. Fortunately the thing hadn't gone far enough that he had actually given rise to any expectation on her part.

He must point out her error gently, if she was actually working under a misapprehension. "It's a brave man who would cross Romeo in public," he replied.

"He is a severe burden on you," she answered sympathetically. "But then he will be returning to Greece soon, I expect."

"I hope not. I enjoy my brother's company. With the proper wife, he will settle down to propriety."

Jane could not control a gurgle of laughter. "Oh, Renfrew!" she said, shaking her head. "He is incorrigible. He had the carriage drawn to a dead halt in heavy traffic yesterday, while he got out and paid tribute to a doorway in Great Ormond Street."

Renfrew was struck with how pretty Jane was when she smiled. "You must own, it was a very handsome doorway," he parried.

"I see this madness is in the family's blood."

"Madness? Let us call it eccentricity, and I contend the proper lady could cure it.'

A flush of pleasure colored her cheeks, and a smile trembled on her lips. Renfrew saw that shy smile, and felt a stab of chagrin at the ambiguity of his speech.

"I don't think you are seriously infected," she said, rather breathlessly. "At least you don't crop out into classical quotations so often as your brother."

The thing to do was highlight Romeo's talents. "My brother is an excellent scholar. I haven't a tenth of his understanding of the classics."

"Less than a tenth is still more than enough."

"These fits of quotations come and go with Romeo. He is actually very clever—and talented! He paints, sculpts, designs buildings. One is never bored in Romeo's company," he said earnestly.

As Miss Halsey was never in Romeo's company except with Lord Renfrew, she could truthfully concur in this assessment. "Indeed, no! Bored is the wrong word. I like him excessively now that I am coming to know him." Renfrew smiled his satisfaction. "And Belle likes him, too," she added.

"It's important for families to get along together—all the members, I mean. It makes the family gatherings more congenial."

This talk of family and family gatherings coming on top of the earlier mention of her dowry sent Jane into spasms of confused delight.

"You must meet Mama soon," Renfrew continued. "My father has returned to Hampshire, but Mama is eager to meet you and Belle, and of course your aunt. Romeo speaks of you so often, she is on thorns to see Pallas Athene for herself."

"I hope he hasn't painted me as a warrior queen!"

"Complete with sword and shield. Mama is having the guns oiled to defend herself."

"Just so she doesn't bar the door." Jane laughed.

"I'll arrange a family meeting soon. You must all come for tea."

It was a night of enchantment for Jane. Hardly more than a week ago she had been wondering what would ever become of her. Now Lord Renfrew, the handsomest, most eligible *parti* in town, was asking her home to meet his mother and speaking of family gatherings. It seemed like a dream. And to add to her pleasure, Belle had begun to show some interest in Romeo. While Romeo did not appeal to Jane, Belle was more lenient in her demands. Romeo was a little strange to be sure, but he was sweet-tempered and very eligible.

"Do you think Romeo really might remain in England if he were happily married?" she asked suddenly. It was the possibility of Belle's marrying him that caused the question.

Renfrew read the interest in her eyes, and encouraged it. "My brother is biddable. If his wife wants it very much, then I think he would."

"That would be nice," she said pensively.

As the waltz came to an end, Renfrew studied Jane's expression. He had been mistaken to think she cared for himself. How conceited he had become, as society's darling. He was surprised to feel a little rankling needle of discontent at the realization that it was Romeo she had favored all along.

"Shall we joint the others?" he suggested. "I haven't stood up with Miss Belle yet. We must begin cementing family bonds," he added archly, as he led her to their party.

"You and I shall perform another salute to Terpsichore," Romeo told Jane.

"Indeed we shall not, sir. We have already honored Terpsichore once this evening."

"Then this time we shall honor ourselves."

"It is my intention to honor my cousin," Jane said, detaching his fingers from her arm and placing her hand on Basil's arm.

Romeo sighed resignedly. "Oh, very well. No harm can come to you with Pettigrew. I shall feel safer than when you dance with James. My brother is so very handsome, and even richer than I. And of course a famous flirt," he added.

There was a moment of awkward silence while everyone except Romeo looked an apology at Basil. Then Jane exchanged a gaze with Renfrew. "Can I trust you with my little sister, sir?" she asked.

"Can I trust you with your cousin?" he replied.

"You can all trust me with the titian-haired beauty in the green gown," Romeo decided. "She has beautiful bosoms, has she not?" He turned an apologetic face to Jane. "But not so beautiful as yours, Athene. Yours are smaller, but firmer. Don't you think, James?"

"Best hurry along before the lady is taken, Romeo," James said, with a damping glare. As Romeo glided forth, Renfrew darted a glance to Jane to see how she had reacted to Romeo's latest outrage. He saw the laughter lurking there, and an answering smile twitched his lips. "Perhaps we were precipitate to hope he will remain in London. One wonders if Greece is not the place for him."

"I can't imagine what you're talking about, Renfrew," Jane said through unsteady lips.

Belle gasped. "Jane! What will Renfrew think of you?"

"I'm sure Renfrew realizes a lady never hears any lewd or objectionable comment. I see nothing amiss in Romeo's standing up with the lady in the green gown. She appears unexceptionable."

Renfrew clapped his hands lightly. "Bravo, Miss

Halsey. I applaud your lack of hearing. That was worthy of a diplomat."

Jane curtsied playfully. "We aging debs make up in diplomacy what we lack in youth."

She stood up next with Basil, and tried to sound him out on how matters stood between him and Belle. "What a pretty couple Romeo and Belle made, dancing together," she said with an air of innocence.

Basil shook his head. "It's you he's interested in, Jane. Any fool can see that. You've scored a double hit. Things will be touchy when Romeo learns you favor his brother."

"Perhaps he'll turn to Belle for sympathy."

"Aye, and perhaps I'll land him a facer if he tries talking about her b—about her body in public."

Jane blinked in surprise. "Are you and Belle—she has said nothing to me about it!"

"I haven't offered for her!" he exclaimed in surprise. "Good God, how could I? Till I put a nest egg aside, I can't offer for anyone. My whole energy at the moment is to establish myself. Mama is always at me to find an heiress. I daresay I ought to be finding out which of the ladies here are rich."

The romance had come off the boil then, Jane concluded, and was relieved to hear it. She must speak to Belle, and hint of the superior life she would live as Lady Romeo. Belle had no outstanding hankering after wealth or titles, but she had been raised in more liberal circumstances than Basil could ever provide, and she would soon feel the pinch after marriage. To see her beautiful sister sunk to being a clerk's wife was painful. The difference in their circumstances would be all the more pronounced if Renfrew offered for herself. Incredible though it was, it seemed that very thing might happen.

When the sisters discussed the party in their room with Miss Munch that night, Jane began planting the idea that Romeo might make a good *parti*.

"I notice you stood up twice with Lord Romeo," Jane said. "He is very amusing, is he not?"

"He is so clever I can hardly talk to him," Belle confessed.

"Renfrew says he is a very learned scholar of the classics. He wishes he had a tenth of Romeo's learning."

Belle gave a bold smile. "It's too bad he's going to Greece, or I might make a push to attach him," she said.

"He'd be better than your cousin," Miss Munch averred. "You'll end up battening yourself on his mother in this shoe box if you take Pettigrew. At your age you ought to have more than one fire in the irons."

"Basil and I are only friends," Belle objected. "Papa had no opinion of first cousins marrying."

Jane and Miss Munch exchanged a satisfied look over her head. "Renfrew was saying Romeo would probably remain in England if his wife wished it," Jane said nonchalantly. "He will make an excellent *parti* for some young lady."

"Yes, some lady like you," Belle pouted. "It is all he speaks of, Jane. I don't know what he'll do when you marry Renfrew."

"He'll find someone to comfort him," Miss Munch threw in slyly.

Jane felt obliged to offer a demur. "Good gracious! Renfrew hasn't offered for me. We've only been out a few times."

"He doesn't want you to meet his mother either, I suppose?" Munch rallied. "I'll press up your best mulled muslin for the visit. Will your aunt be going as well?"

"Yes, the whole family," Jane replied.

"Then I'll get at your gowns early, or I'll not be able to get near the iron. It's like working in a cubbyhole, trying to squeeze an ironing board up in that kitchen. It's a good thing I'm a pygmy."

Miss Munch left, and Jane and Belle continued discussing the party. "Wouldn't it be fine if you married Romeo, and I married Renfrew?" Jane said, as she brushed out her hair at the mirror. "We would live close to each other in Hampshire."

Belle took her brush to the bed. "But Romeo really does not care for me in the least, Jane. You are his ideal, and we are quite different. It seems the more you bark at him, the better he likes you."

"Then perhaps you should learn to bark," Jane suggested.

"Perhaps I shall."

Chapter Five

RENFREW HAD a few qualms that he was doing his brother more harm than good by being so often with Miss Halsey, and decided it was time Romeo do his own courting. The Corn Bill was being debated in the House in any case, and as he was on the committee, he should be there.

"Must you?" his mother asked, when he explained his afternoon's plan. "It seems a shame to risk losing Miss Halsey, after all your work."

"She's warming up to Romeo. Last evening she showed a deal of interest in his remaining in England. I think it's time to cut the pair of them loose."

"The very thought of setting Romeo loose sends shivers up my spine. But Miss Halsey is a firm sort of young lady, you said?"

"Yes, quite firm. She'll do, Mama."

When the door knocker on Catherine Street sounded that afternoon, it was only Lord Romeo who was shown in. After a formal bow to his hostess, he looked around and shook his head at the size and quality of the room. He was familiar with it by this time, but it never failed to depress him to see Athene in such squalid surroundings, like a diamond set in lead.

"I really must get you out of here immediately," he murmured in Jane's direction, but his murmurings were by no means inaudible to her aunt.

"You are eager to get us into the sunlight," Jane said for her aunt's benefit, and rushed on to forestall a contradiction. "Where is Renfrew today?"

"James is speaking in the House. It has something to do with corn and money."

"Then he won't be with us?" Jane's eyes moved consideringly from Romeo to Belle, and she said, "Perhaps I'll remain home today." This would give her sister a free hand with Romeo.

Romeo looked crestfallen. "You sound as though it is only Renfrew whose company you enjoy!"

"Don't be absurd. I enjoy your company, too, Romeo, but we have been trotting pretty hard, and I am not so young as you."

Romeo bristled up to his full height and announced, "I am nearly twenty-six! I appear younger, which is a curse, but as we all age, it will be to my advantage."

Jane took up a magazine and said, "Why don't you go out with Romeo, Belle?"

Romeo's innocent blue eyes narrowed into slits. "Yes, you would like to hear James speak in the House, would you not, Miss Belle?"

Jane's magazine fell from her fingers. She looked at Romeo, and saw on his face an expression worthy of wily Odysseus. A smile of capitulation grew, and she said, "We shall all go. It won't be so very tiring, just sitting in the House for an hour or so."

"My thoughts exactly," Romeo replied.

Jane was only amused at the incident. She assumed James had sent Romeo to deliver her. When they went to the carriage, it was not Renfrew's stately chaise that awaited them, but a bizarre concoction of Romeo's own design. It was a straw garden carriage with a blue silk overhead parasol, which might have been amusing in the country or quite at home at Astley's Circus, but appeared ludicrous in London. A pair of frisky cream ponies were in the harness, pawing the ground in their eagerness to be off.

"I designed this for you, Athene," he said, smiling at his creation. "You and Phaëthon, to commemorate his driving the chariot of the sun."

"How lovely," Jane said, stifling her laughter.

"Isn't it sweet!" Belle exclaimed. "Look, Jane! The squabs are watered silk, and the fittings are gold!"

"Brass actually," Romeo said. "James thought gold would be ostentatious. We wouldn't want to draw attention to ourselves. That would be vulgar."

Jane thought they would have a vulgar amount of attention even without gold fittings. The squawking of the straw as they took up their seats was enough to cause heads to turn.

As Romeo assisted them into the rig, Belle continued extolling its virtues. "And the ponies—so perfectly matched they look like twins. How I should love to take the reins."

"If you ask me very nicely, I might permit it, for Jane's sister, but not in traffic," Romeo told her. Then he turned to Jane. "I was hoping you would condescend to take the ribbons, Jane. You don't mind if I call you Jane?"

"Actually I prefer it to Athene."

"I consider Athene a title, like Countess, or Duchess. Mama says it is a sign of poor breeding to be using first names too soon. There can be no question of *my* breeding, however, and James tells me your own papa was a baronet, so I think we may dispense with the formality without fear of appearing underbred."

"Let us consider it settled," Jane said. "What time is Renfrew speaking?"

"He is scheduled for two, which means not before three. We don't want to arrive too early. The seats are deuced hard, and all the lords are long-winded."

By constant harping, Jane managed to keep Romeo from such temptations as the classical doorway on Great Ormond Street, so they arrived at Westminster before three. By the time they had taken their seat in the dusty aerie set under the eaves for visitors, Renfrew was already speaking. Jane sat like a statue, admiring his appearance, and listening to every word. His voice, echoing in the vast hall, sounded vastly impressive, but the speech was so complicated, she had very little idea what he was recommending. She felt her ignorance, and determined to have Renfrew explain the Corn Laws to her at the first opportunity.

When he sat down, there was a burst of applause from the Whig side of the House. Romeo rose immediately and said, "Shall we go now?"

"Are we not waiting for Renfrew?" Jane asked, surprised.

"He may be here till seven or eight," Romeo told her, and took her arm to lead her downstairs. "Poor James, spending such a lovely day in that medieval torture chamber. I really should rescue him."

"Why don't you send in a note with a page, and let him know we're here?" Jane suggested at once.

"He wouldn't appreciate being interrupted at his work. James actually takes the Corn Laws seriously."

Lord Renfrew had no idea his brother was bringing the ladies to the House, nor did he spot them in the visitors' gallery. But after his speech, he wanted to walk away his nervous energy and went outside, where he met the visitors waiting for their carriage.

"Romeo! What are you doing here!" he exclaimed.

Jane heard his exclamation with surprise. Had he not asked Romeo to bring her? She felt awkward, as if she had come uninvited to a party.

"I wanted to show Jane I am interested in serious matters," he said frankly. "Unfortunately I couldn't keep up the pretense, but I remembered your teaching me the most important thing a member of Parliament must learn. It was very useful during your speech."

"What is that?" Belle asked.

"I did manage to yawn without opening my mouth," Romeo said.

Jane caught Renfrew's eye and smiled. "I am flattered," James said, with a bow.

"Your speech was wonderful, Renfrew," Jane said. "I didn't understand it completely. I hope you will explain it to me sometime."

Renfrew was flattered and said, "I would be happy to."

"Ah, here is my carriage," Romeo exclaimed, as his rig was led forth.

Renfrew, who had heard much of the carriage,

but not actually seen it before, stood agape. "What in God's name is that!"

Romeo smiled softly. "It quite takes the breath away, does it not? I have seen nothing like it, even in Greece. I used a design from an old amphora as the model, improved by myself. The parasol is my own contrivance. Unfortunately the rig squawks like the devil, but the ladies were kind enough to pretend they didn't notice. Would you like to try it, James?"

"Thank you, no."

"Good. I felt I ought to offer, but I doubt if it is up to your weight. I am taking the ladies for a drive, to blow away the cobwebs of Westminster. You won't be coming, then, I take it?"

Jane listened with interest for his answer. Renfrew gazed at the sun gleaming in the cloudless sky, felt the warm zephyr fan his cheek, and decided he had done his duty by England and his brother for that day. Feeling happy with himself and the world, he decided he had earned a modest reward, and an afternoon with two handsome young ladies and his brother appealed strongly to him. And really he wasn't sure Romeo ought to be left entirely on his own with Jane till he had firmly attached her. "Why not? I'll have my chaise brought around. Where are we going?"

"Somewhere to hear the water murmur," Romeo replied. "We shall examine the new stone bridge they are naming after Wellington's victory. Waterloo Bridge, I hear they are to call it. Canova, the Italian sculptor, says it is worth the trip from Rome. I find that hard to believe, but satisfying our curiosity is worth the trip across town. No doubt the commissions Canova has received from the Prince Regent skewed his artistic judgment."

"The *on-dit* at Westminster is that it is Prinny's paying for returning the Apollo Belvedere to Italy that accounts for Canova's generous opinion," Renfrew explained.

"How informative to have a brother in the halls of power." Romeo smiled. "It makes me feel as if I know what is going forth in the world. One is so often at a loss to understand bizarre reality. Why do you not get some commissions for me, James?"

"If you were definitely remaining in England, I might do something in that line," Renfrew tempted.

Romeo could never keep his attention long from Jane, and was soon back pestering her. "Will you take the reins of my gig, Jane?" Renfrew looked a little startled to hear the couple were on a first-name basis. "We have successfully vaulted the hurdle of Miss and Lord," Romeo explained aside.

"Belle wanted to give it a try," Jane reminded him.

"But I would like *you* to drive me," he insisted gently.

She declined with a polite smile. "I would prefer not to, Romeo."

"It is the squawking that repulses you. It does considerable damage to my own ears. I shall have that rectified before trying to tempt you once again. James, will you be so kind as to bring Jane to Waterloo Bridge for me?"

James had little choice but to agree, and soon his carriage was delivered. Jane settled comfortably into a normal conveyance. "What a goose your brother is," she said. "I fear that straw carriage will prove useless in England's damp climate."

"I was astonished to see it had turned to straw. It is a tribute to Phaëthon, and should by rights be made of precious metal. Romeo is familiar with all the details of antiquity. Quite an accomplished scholar," he said.

Jane smiled. "I see you attempt to dilute his folly by dragging in antiquity. He mentioned Phaëthon. I don't believe I'm familiar with that gentleman's carriage. I cannot believe it had much in common with today's phaetons, despite the name."

"Phaëthon was the son of Helios, the sun god, but his chums laughed when he said so. To prove it, he asked a favor of his father—that Helios let him drive the chariot of the sun, which turned night into day. To make a long and very silly story short, poor Phaëthon ran amok. We may count ourselves fortunate Romeo didn't try to create a reproduction of Hephaestus' work—all gold and silver and diamonds."

"Now I see your trick. Romeo told me you convinced him gold trim would be vulgar."

Renfrew and Jane exchanged a conspiratorial smile. "And expensive! Soon he will have two of us preaching thrift and common sense in his ear."

"And now let *us* talk common sense, if you please," Jane declared. "I felt so ignorant during your speech. I thought the price of corn had been settled at eighty shillings the bushel. What is causing this new rise in price?"

James outlined the complications of currency legislation and excess issuing of paper money that caused the fluctuations. He was flattered at her interest, and well-impressed with her questions. He was happy to discover Romeo's bride-to-be had such serious interests.

"It's unusual to find a lady interested in this sort of thing," he mentioned, and Jane swelled with pleasure.

Before she quite understood the intricacies of the

problem, they found themselves at Waterloo Bridge, where the finishing touches were being applied, preparatory to its grand opening on the anniversary of Waterloo. There were still workmen on the bridge, and some working from barges below.

"It's beautiful, so light and airy; it's hard to believe it's made of stone," Belle exclaimed.

"I wish I could admire it," Renfrew said, with a smile hinting at some joke.

"Is it not classical enough to please you?" Jane asked. "That is more usually your brother's objection to everything."

"On the contrary, I admire the design. No, what I am honor-bound to object to is its being made of stone. There was a great debate in Parliament as to whether it should be of stone or wood. My group came down on the side of wood. We were known as the Wooden Peers. I deny to the death that it was any slur on the composition of our heads."

"It's unlike you to cast your vote on the wrong side, Renfrew," Jane exclaimed. "Surely stone is more enduring."

"That's a flattering assessment of my judgment—and true," he added with a conning smile. "But at the time my committee on the Corn Laws needed the support of a certain group of gentlemen who favored the cheaper wooden bridge. It is known as the art of compromise."

"You *do* occasionally lose, then, do you?" she said, with a flirtatious glance.

"Almost always—in politics. I am a Whig, you see, and the Tories rule the roost at Westminster."

Romeo's eyes narrowed suspiciously as he listened to this exchange. "James, you are flirting with Jane," he said baldly. "I knew how it would be when you decided to join us. Go and talk to Belle."

James made a playful bow to Miss Halsey. "Guilty as charged," he said. "I daresay you didn't recognize a treatise on politics as flirtation, Miss Halsey."

"If it was politics you were discussing, I acquit you of anything but bad taste," Romeo decided. "It is unlike you to do anything so tedious. And furthermore your eyes were sparkling."

James and Jane exchanged a smile. "Take care or I shall be wooing you with a dissertation on the Whigs' planned financial legislation," he cautioned.

"Another time," Jane said, answering his bow with a graceful curtsy. "Now I fear I am going to be courted in the Grecian style."

Romeo took Jane's arm and led her a little away from the others. He stood, gazing out over the Thames. "You are looking at the gateway to freedom," he said, in solemn tones. "If you and I were to board one of those barges, we might sail down the coast of France and Portugal, through the Strait of Gilbralter to the Mediterranean. There is nothing like it, Jane."

"A barge all the way to the Mediterranean! That would not be very comfortable. Besides, I like England, Romeo. I wish you would give up this notion of returning to Greece."

"You've never known anything but this foggy, dismal isle. You have no standard with which to compare it. Picture a crystal blue sky, and on a distant hill, the stately columns of the Parthenon. I must ask James what his friends had to say about my buying the Elgin Marbles." He turned and walked away from Jane, who was not slow to follow him to Renfrew.

"Did you have any luck in putting my proposition regarding buying Elgin's stolen marbles to the government?" Romeo asked.

"I didn't get that far, Romeo," Renfrew admitted. "My own colleagues laughed me out of the room when I suggested it. I fear you must forget that notion of buying the Elgin Marbles. Look on the bright side—you've saved fifty thousand pounds."

"I've lost the battle, not the war," Romeo informed him. "Shall we go over to Burlington House and visit Pettigrew? I want to broach a matter to him."

No one expressed much interest in this scheme, but Jane could not like to prohibit it, and with his usual bland insistence, Romeo got them into the carriages. On this occasion, he persuaded Jane to accompany him.

"What is it you want to discuss with my cousin?" she asked. "The Elgin Marbles are not his to sell, you must know. He is only in charge of them."

"If James says they are not for sale, then they are not for sale. He is one of those men who always knows things. I am a little peeved with him today, but there is no point in denying facts. I just want to speak to Pettigrew about how the Marbles are being shipped to the British Museum. Elgin busted them up so badly, special precautions must be taken in the removal from Burlington House."

Basil was in his office. While the rest of the party took another look at the exhibit, Romeo went to visit him, and made quite a pest of himself by insisting he be shown what sort of wrappings were to be used, and where the artifacts were to be stored while awaiting the remove.

"Are you sure the building is secure?" Romeo demanded.

"The doors are inches thick, and there is a guard on duty day and night," Basil explained.

"Where does he take up his guard at night?"

"He patrols the front of the building."

"And if someone should get in via a window?"

"The guard has a key. He makes tours every hour on the hour. You can rest assured we are taking no chances, Lord Romeo."

"Who else has a key?"

"Only myself, and a few of the other employees."

"I hope you keep the key safe on you at all times?"

"It doesn't leave my pocket."

"I don't suppose you take it out with you in the evening?"

"No, I usually leave it on my dresser, but then I doubt if anyone is going to break into my bedroom and steal it."

After a dozen more prying questions, Lord Romeo appeared satisfied and returned to his party. "We shall take the ladies home now, James," he announced. "We are taking them to a rout party this evening, and they will want to put their hair up in papers and smear things on their faces to look pretty," he explained to his brother.

"It is indeed a full-time job to turn out in decent looks so frequently," Jane agreed through unsteady lips.

"I don't have to do my hair up in papers!" Belle objected.

Romeo examined her idly. "Is it naturally curly?"

"Yes."

"Pity. I like a touch of art in my ladies. That hint of the courtesan is highly erotic to me. I have nothing against a discreet daub of rouge, and I adore perfume."

"What kind of perfume?" Belle asked eagerly.

"That must depend on the lady. For someone like you, a flower scent would suffice. An Athene requires musk."

"I shan't inquire why," Jane said warily.

"A heavier, more voluptuous scent would better suit a lady of your years. Flower scents are for girls. All my hetaerae wear musk."

"What are your hetaerae?" Belle asked.

"I don't believe we want to know," Jane cautioned.

Romeo gave his explanation to Belle. "The origin of the word is *hetairos*, Greek for 'comrade in arms,' a military term," Romeo explained. "Change one of the comrades from male to female, the setting from war to love, and the definition might still stand. You must not think I am discussing common prostitutes, however."

Jane directed a commanding glance toward Renfrew, who tried to stop his brother's explanation. "Let us be going now, Romeo. The ladies don't want to hear this."

"Don't be missish, James. You must know young ladies love a naughty discussion, so long as one keeps at least a superficial air of propriety. We are discussing Greek customs. What could be more unexceptionable? As I was saying, ladies, a hetaera is much more than a doxy, she is an intellectual companion and friend and lover in one. Mine invariably wear musk. For me, still carrying the burden of my English upbringing, the scent of musk has an aura of sin that is irresistible. Wear musk tonight, Athene."

"I don't own any musk, and am not likely to purchase any after what you have said. And in future I would thank you not to discuss prostitutes in front of me and my sister."

Romeo stiffened. "I expected better of you, Athene. I do you an honor to treat you as an equal, instead of a second-class citizen, as most men treat their women. Which is more degrading to your sex— to carry on with the muslin company behind your backs like James and his friends, or to deal frankly?"

Nine-tenths of his tirade was ignored. "Like James?" she asked, her head turning to Renfrew. Her stormy eyes demanded an explanation.

"I see that arrow hit its mark!" Romeo crowed.

Renfrew felt an overpowering urge to box his brother's ears. "We'll discuss this later, Romeo," he said stiffly. "Miss Belle, may I have the pleasure of escorting you home?"

"I'm not traveling alone in that straw basket with Romeo!" Jane declared, and joined her sister and Renfrew.

Romeo watched them all leave. He didn't return to his own carriage, but clambered down the bank of the Thames and hailed a bargeman. "Where could I buy one of these barges?" he asked.

"Now what would you want one of these for, laddie?" the man asked. "These are only for hauling a heavy load."

"It happens I have to haul a heavy load across the ocean."

"Nay, this is no ship. You'd be swamped on the high seas with this little raft."

"I believe you're right. For the high seas I shall need a proper ship. One that can carry a good deal of weight. Something like an East India Company frigate, or even a warship. But I can hardly ap-

proach the Admiralty . . . I'll go to the East India
Company. Thank you for your assistance, sir."

"Any time, lad."

Inside Lord Renfrew's carriage, a heavy silence
lay over the occupants. Jane's mind was afire with
conjecture. How calmly Romeo had mentioned Renfrew's lightskirts, and James hadn't even denied it!
Renfrew sat scowling into his lap. Romeo was incorrigible! All his careful work in promoting his
brother's romance was on its way out the window.
And that wasn't the only thing that bothered him.
There were some people whose good opinion he
cherished, and Miss Halsey was of that class. She
was a nice woman, decent, respectable. It galled
him that Romeo had given her such an unflattering
picture of him.

Belle looked from one to the other and decided
she must smooth this rough patch up, for Jane's
sake. It was Renfrew's sins that bothered her sister, but Romeo's would do to get them speaking to
each other.

"He didn't mean any harm, you know," she said
tentatively. "It was odd of him to speak of those
hetaerae in front of ladies, but it is only his way.
Romeo always speaks without thinking. It is one of
his charms really."

"Charms?" Jane snorted.

"You are losing your sense of humor, Jane," Belle
chided softly.

"Immorality is not a source of amusement to me."

Belle blushed to her ears and said diffidently,
"Bachelors behave differently from married men.
Once a man is married, he often settles down." She
peered at Renfrew as she spoke.

He scowled her into silence, and the carriage continued on its way toward Catherine Street. At the

door, Renfrew descended to accompany the ladies to the house.

Again it was Belle who spoke. "We enjoyed your speech very much, Lord Renfrew. Didn't we, Jane?" she prodded.

"Yes, your *speech* was excellent, Renfrew," Jane sniped. "*It* even showed some semblance of conscience."

Without further ado, Renfrew said, "Would you mind leaving us a moment, Miss Belle? I'd like to speak to your sister privately."

Belle ran into the house, and Jane found herself alone with Renfrew. "What is it you have to say?" she asked stiffly.

"You're being unfair to judge me on hearsay evidence, and that from a man who actually knows very little about my private life."

Jane leveled a cool stare on him. "But was it true?"

"I'm thirty years old, and a bachelor. What do you think?"

Jane showed her opinion by an angry toss of her head. "I don't believe it's proper for us—Belle and myself—to be keeping company with roués. You will excuse us from attending the rout with you this evening, Lord Renfrew."

"Roués! Good God, woman, did you take me for a saint?"

"No, I took you for a gentleman!" she sniped, and turned to leave.

Renfrew reached out and grabbed her wrist to stop her. He told himself he was doing it for Romeo, but lurking at the bottom of his heart, unexamined, was a different reason. The stab of anger and regret at her curt dismissal was not the reaction of a mere disinterested observer.

"I don't have a mistress," he said angrily.

Jane studied him for a moment. He watched, bewitched as her scowl turned slowly to a smile. "You might have told me so, James," she said, and laughed.

She read an answering smile in Renfrew's blue eyes. "You'll come with us tonight?" he asked.

"Yes, sans musk," she replied, and ran up the stairs.

Belle was waiting in their bedroom. "What did he say?" she demanded.

"He doesn't have a mistress." She smiled. "I believe he had, in the past, but so long as he hasn't one now, I can forgive that."

"Oh, I'm so glad! I was afraid you were going to give him his congé. And just when I am making some headway with Romeo. He told me that with a proper mentor, I might become something more than a dull girl. Was that not flattering?"

"I wonder what mentor he had in mind?"

"It hasn't occurred to him yet that the job is his for the asking. Perhaps when Renfrew makes his offer to you, he will come up to scratch. Oh, they are lovely, aren't they, Jane? I never really believed we would pull it off, both of us nab a *parti*."

"We haven't pulled it off yet, my girl." But Belle had put Basil behind her, and that was a good first step.

Munch listened eagerly, and finally added her mite. "Romeo's a slow top if he don't nab a pretty girl like Missie when he gets the chance. But with him being a knock-in-the-cradle, you might have to draw him a pitcher. I don't know which of you is doing better: Miss Halsey landing a marquess, or Missie having the luck to nab a rich idiot. You can play ducks and drakes with his fortune, and he'll never know the difference."

In his carriage, Renfrew was less jubilant as he reviewed the meeting. Why had Miss Halsey ripped up at him? Her anger should have been directed toward Romeo, but it was his own innocence she wanted to hear. Was it possible she thought he was dangling after her young sister? He had noticed an outcropping of that protective streak before. He was being rapidly painted into a corner here. Belle was his main means of throwing Romeo and Jane together. She was the other partner in the foursome, and he spent considerable time with her, perforce. The chit didn't seem to have any unusual affection for him ... though today she had leapt to his defense with unusual alacrity. Oh, lord, that was all he needed, an infatuated youngster to cope with.

But it was worth the bother. Romeo was insane about Miss Halsey. How fine it would be to have him shackled to a strong-willed, clever woman. The thing to do was back out of the foursome by degrees. Let Romeo take over. Then he remembered Jane's compliments on his speech, and wondered if it had been her idea to come to the House to hear him. Romeo had not said he was coming. Miss Halsey, Jane, must have suggested it. A frown creased his brow.

Chapter Six

"WHYEVER do you want your nice curls screwed up into a knot for?" Miss Munch demanded, when Belle requested that style for the Nicolsons' rout party.

"Because I want to look classical," Belle said.

"If it's class you're after, take a look at your sister. There is class."

"Romeo prefers a knot to curls."

"Your Lord Romeo sounds like a strange bird to me, liking a scrubwoman's hairdo. How about you, Miss Halsey? Will you want to be borrowing my blue cotton gown?"

"Certainly not. Renfrew has no preference for such oddities. I shall wear my jonquil silk, with the green ribbons—and my flowered scent," she added with a secret smile.

"Then you'll be wearing your green kid slippers. May I borrow your silver ones?" Belle asked.

Miss Munch's heart swelled with pride when her girls sallied forth, fine as stars, despite the knot that adorned Belle's head. Aye, it would take more than a knot to put a blight on that one's beauty. Basil was accompanying his mama to a concert that evening, but they were both in attendance when the gentlemen arrived. Mrs. Pettigrew planned to praise Basil's industry as much as possible in the five minutes they all sat together.

Despite Belle's best efforts, Romeo remained blind to the charms of a Psyche hairdo. His comment, addressed to Jane, was, "I don't smell any musk, Athene." He next turned his attention to Basil.

"Ah, Pettigrew! May I call you Herb?"

Basil blinked behind his spectacles. "I beg your pardon?"

"Did they not tell you? We are all on a first-name basis now."

"But my name is Basil."

"Just so. A herb of the mint family, I believe? We use a deal of it at home. In Greece, I mean, obviously. England limits itself to salt and pepper and mustard. Basil, I shall endeavor to remember that. I am studying mnemonics in my spare time. I have achieved only partial success thus far, but I knew you were an herb of some sort."

Renfrew managed to divert the conversation to the party, and Romeo's foolishness passed with only minimal confusion.

In the carriage, Romeo undertook an explanation of his lapse. "I hope I haven't offended Basil. I am particularly anxious to be in his good books, for I have a favor to request of him."

"What is that, Romeo?" Belle asked.

"Thalia. I feel her head must have fallen somewhere in the lumber of Burlington House, for I found her body this afternoon. I returned to the

Marbles after you all ran off on me. I would like permission to search around for the head. I dislike envisioning poor Thalia headless into the stretch of eternity. Could Basil arrange that small favor for me?"

"I expect he would be happy for any help you could give in putting the bits and pieces together," Jane replied.

This seemed a safe diversion for the bothersome young gentleman, and everyone lauded his intention. Belle even offered to assist him. "If you can coerce Athene to accompany you," he said blandly. "Otherwise, I shan't want a babbling girl distracting me."

It was always a touchy moment, claiming partners for the first dance. Renfrew, on his best behavior, made a point of asking Belle to stand up with him for the opening minuet, but her sister didn't mind. It prolonged the pleasurable anticipation of dancing with James, and Jane preferred to have a waltz with him. She could not blame Renfrew for missing the next set. Romeo insisted he had forgotten dinner, and drew Jane along to the refreshment parlor with him.

"You are nearly perfect, Athene, but I wish to see another stone on you. Try some of this lobster. It has the reputation of being an aphrodisiac."

Jane was uncertain of his meaning, and took it for some more classical nonsense. "A pity they don't know how to prepare it," Romeo said, after his first sampling. He set the dish aside with a grimace and selected a clump of grapes from a carefully arranged centerpiece. "But then what can one expect of a nation that considers cabbage fit for human consumption? The lobster has been boiled to death."

"I should hope so!"

"Ah, you are endeavoring to make a joke. Yes, live lobster would hardly be palatable either. All the same, I shall speak to the hostess."

"I shouldn't bother with that, Romeo," Jane told him. "In England, we like it this way."

"Yes, England excels at overcooking seafood to a pulp. I suppose you will want to find a partner for the next dance" was his next speech.

"I wonder where Renfrew and Belle are."

Romeo's eyes narrowed, and he set down his plate. "Or shall we find a quiet corner and talk instead? Yes, that would be better. I saw a library as we were shown in. It had a fireplace, but if we sit with our backs to it, we might be quite comfortable."

"Are you chilly?"

"No, I am fevered with desire for you. I hold Adam in such aversion I cannot tolerate to view his works, which have destroyed so many homes in England. It was an Adam fireplace," he condemned.

"Then we certainly shan't sit in that room," Jane said, and used it as an excuse to return to the party.

By the time they reached the ballroom, Renfrew had chosen another partner, and Belle was standing up with a gentleman presented to her by Mrs. Nicolson. The hostess, feeling sorry for Miss Halsey, found her a partner also, and Romeo went alone to the library, where he girded his loins to confront the Adam fireplace and undertake the monumental task of mentally redesigning it. For some forty minutes he became lost in an artistic reverie.

While he dreamed of Grecian improvements, Jane at last got her wish of standing up with Renfrew. He came to her for the waltz, but gave very little pleasure when his first speech was a query as to Romeo's whereabouts.

"You sound as though he needs a keeper," she

scolded. Not a word of praise had she heard on her jonquil gown, or her hairdo.

This idea had to be talked down immediately. "A keeper?" he laughed. "Hardly!" Then he spoiled it by a worried question as to exactly what Romeo was doing.

"Complaining about a fireplace in the library."

Renfrew waltzed his companion toward the edge of the floor, and soon out the door. Jane was prey to delightful conjectures. Was he going to propose? Why else did he want privacy? Perhaps that was why he had seemed a little distracted this evening.

"Which room is the library?" he asked.

She pointed. Renfrew crept up silently and peeped in. He felt a calming wave of relief when he saw Romeo's bleached curls against the sofa. He had rather thought his brother might be at the mantel-piece with a screwdriver. He had quite ruined the Adam fixtures at Stapford House.

"That's all right, then," he sighed. "And now we shall enjoy what remains of this waltz."

Jane wore a peculiar expression as he gathered her into his arms. It was a mixture of curiosity and amusement and anticipation. It lit her eyes, and lent a breathless quality to her speech. "You were frightened, Renfrew; admit it," she teased.

"No, only concerned. Romeo is behaving much better, under your stern guidance."

"I—*stern*?" She laughed. "What a forbidding character you give me. You must remember, it is only on matters of morals that I become stern."

Renfrew smiled, too, at this gentle reminder. "And even then you were not so very stern, so long as the sinner had mended his ways."

"Which, of course, you have," she added, and bated him with a flash from her dark eyes. "Should there not have been a mention in there of repenting?"

"And of never transgressing again," he agreed.

It was not the former transgressions that bothered Renfrew, but the prickling of infatuation he felt as he held his brother's chosen lady in his arms. The air quickened when he was with her. When they were apart, his thoughts often flew to her. His senses seemed preternaturally alert this evening. How lightly she moved. How brightly her eyes sparkled, and how very much he wanted to kiss her. Damn, he was experiencing spring fever. Every spring he suffered through one of these infatuations. Fortunately they were always short-lived. He would not let an infatuation interfere with his plan. He damped down temptation, but his arms tightened insensibly as they whirled to the enchanting rhythm of the waltz.

"I'm giddy with all this spinning." Jane laughed. Her pearl-white teeth gleamed.

"Romeo says the waltz is indecent. He adores it."

"He would."

"So do I."

Their eyes met and held. A silent message passed. Jane felt they were not discussing the waltz. By God, she feels it too, Renfrew thought, and was chagrined with the knowledge. But it was a delightful sensation. Inevitable, soaring, reeling—and appalling. Romeo! No, he was imagining he was in love. It was the wine, and the waltz. It was infatuation, nothing more. It would pass. But he must cease seeing Jane, or he would really be in the suds.

Jane experienced that probing gaze into her eyes as close to a declaration of love. It was a magical moment. She felt heady, intoxicated with the music and the dancing, and the pressure of Renfrew's arms holding her. They swirled around the room, and eventually back toward the door to the hallway.

Wrapped in their emotions, neither noticed Romeo had come to the doorway and stood in an attitude of frozen disapproval, glaring at them. Perfidy was the word in his mind. To think his own brother should be so heartless. The instant the music ended, Romeo marched stiffly into the room and took hold of Renfrew's elbow. His face was white, and in that impassive mask, his blue eyes glittered.

"You will excuse us, Athene. We have matters to discuss, this—gentleman?—and I." He pulled Renfrew down the hall toward a door, and Renfrew went, as he had no desire for a public confrontation.

"I'll be back shortly" was all he said. Then the brothers went out the door, into a small hedged garden.

Jane stood, too astonished at first to speak, or move. She had never seen Romeo in such a state. She was accustomed to thinking of him as a bad joke, but in his present mood, he looked capable of any violence. Belle saw her sister standing alone in the hall and joined her. Within seconds, Belle was apprised of the situation.

"We must go and stop them," she exclaimed, and headed for the door.

Jane first tried to deter her, then decided to go along. In her mind, she kept hearing that demeaning "gentleman?"—and feared what might transpire. Even a duel seemed possible. Men were so foolish about their honor. The hallway was in darkness. The door opened silently, concealing their exit.

Renfrew had led Romeo as far from the house as possible. They stood in the darkest corner of the garden, nearly invisible. It was by the triangle of their white shirtfronts that Jane spotted them in the shadows. They stood together, but it was not a brotherly posture. There was hostility in the air. It was Romeo who spoke, in his clear, fluting voice.

"You are trying to steal my woman, James. Don't deny it."

Renfrew's reply was low-pitched, placating, and inaudible. He must do the right, the proper, the only gentlemanly thing, and deny any interest whatsoever in Jane.

"You knew from the beginning I wanted Jane. Pray do not make it necessary for me to challenge you," Romeo said angrily.

Belle gasped and made a motion of going forward. Jane held her elbow. "No, wait!" she said.

"Remember, I broke Spiro's wrist in Greece," Romeo continued. "I would do no less to my own brother, if it should come to a case of necessity."

"Wrestling!" Belle whispered, and swallowed a snicker of laughter. The awful solemnity of Romeo's manner and words was rendered absurd by his meaning.

Romeo continued. "As a man, you know, I revert to the animal when it is a matter of sex. Note the ram, butting his opponent to oblivion. I saw a billy goat in Greece take an enormous bite from his opponent's haunch, and the nanny goat in question was not even pretty."

"No ramming or biting will be necessary. She's all yours," Renfrew replied at once. "Jane Halsey is nothing to me. I only see her to put your cause forward. *You* are the one who begged me to tag along on these outings. I have better things to do, I promise you."

Jane was astonished at Renfrew's words. "She's

all yours." To hear herself disposed of in this cav-
alier fashion, especially when she had thought Renfrew cared for her, was demeaning in the extreme.
Renfrew didn't care for her. It was all a misunderstanding. And there was worse to come.

"Then perhaps it is time you quit chasing after
her," Romeo said.

"The shoe is on the other foot. Try if you can get
her to stop hounding me. Don't drag her down to
the House when I have gone there for the purpose
of escaping her."

Romeo's shoulders fell. "That was partly my
fault. I fear there is something in what you say,
James. She wouldn't come out with me till I had
the inspiration of going to hear you speak. But you
were flirting with her that day. I could see it in
your eyes."

"What you saw was frustration. I've had enough
of this three-cornered romance. You're on your own,
brother."

"I see it now," Romeo said, his voice softening.
"You have been trying to make me jealous to in-
crease my ardor for her. Such ruses are contemptible, and unnecessary. Jane will never belong totally
to any man. That is what I adore about her, that
bellicose spirit. What a challenge to bring her under my thumb. I shall quite insist she treat me as
her lord and master, of course, but I shall be a
tender master."

Jane had heard enough. "Lord and master indeed!" she growled, and darted back into the house,
followed by Belle. Her mind whirled with insults.
Renfrew accused her of chasing him, and there was
just enough truth in it to cause a fever of humiliation. She had taken his infatuation for granted.

How could she have been such a fool? Her only thought was to escape, never to see Renfrew again.

"I fear it is hopeless for me," Belle said forlornly. "Romeo doesn't care for me in the least."

"Nor Renfrew for me! What a take-in. All he wanted was a keeper for that lunatic brother."

"I really don't feel up to remaining at this party, but how shall we get home?" Belle said wearily.

"Don't worry, sister. I'll manage it. My tender master can have no objection to my calling his carriage."

With flashing eye, Jane had the brothers' carriage called, and told Mrs. Nicolson Belle had a touch of migraine. She would have the carriage returned, and perhaps the hostess would be kind enough to tell Lord Renfrew they had to leave early. No need to interrupt the gentlemen's pleasure. She believed the gentlemen had stepped out to blow a cloud. Mrs. Nicolson was relieved not to be losing such prime *partis* as Renfrew and Lord Romeo from her rout, and promised she would give the message.

Unfortunately, she caught a glimpse of Renfrew before the carriage came to the door, and explained the situation. "Where are the ladies? I shall accompany them home," Renfrew said at once.

"They are waiting in the library."

Renfrew hastened forward, all unaware that his argument with Romeo had been overheard. He saw the ladies sitting on the sofa together.

"Miss Belle, I'm sorry to hear you're not feeling well," he said, as he advanced quickly toward them.

One blast from Jane's stormy eyes told him there was more than a migraine to contend with. Her face wouldn't be as white as snow over Belle's headache. She wouldn't be rigid, almost trembling with anger. "What happened?" he demanded, but already had an inkling of the awful truth.

Jane leveled an arctic stare and said "Nothing" in a voice like white ice.

"You heard us—"

"Your little conversation in the garden with Romeo, do you mean? Yes, we overheard a word or two. The words 'hounding,' 'trying to escape.' Good God, you make me sound like a bailiff! I never pursued you!"

"Jane, I'm sorry." His hands went out to her spontaneously, and Jane pulled back.

"Don't you dare touch me! The arrogance, the conceit, to think I was *chasing* you! I wouldn't have you on a platter, and that goes for your lunatic brother as well."

"It was all a misunderstanding."

"Was it indeed? Do I misunderstand to think you were trying to con me into marrying that bedlamite, to stand guard over him so the world would not learn he is as queer as Dick's hatband? I fear the whole Stapford family is similarly afflicted if you think for one instant I would ever consider an offer of marriage from any of you!"

Renfrew damped down his rising anger. "I'll take you home. This business would be better discussed in private."

"There is nothing to discuss," Jane said haughtily, and turned her head away from the sight of her degradation.

At that inopportune moment, a servant came to the door and announced the carriage.

"Come along," Renfrew said.

"If you dare to accompany us out the door, we shall walk home," Jane said. Her glare told Renfrew she was prepared to execute this threat.

"I shall call on you tomorrow."

"Don't you ever darken the door of Catherine Street again."

On this uncompromising speech, Jane rose and strode from the room. Belle looked an apology over her shoulder to Renfrew and followed after her.

Belle was sniffling in the carriage. Jane felt like bawling, too, but tears were not her style. She fumed impotently instead. "To think of the deceit, the treachery, of Renfrew. 'She's all yours,' he said, as though I were his private property, to dispose of as he wished. He *never* cared for me."

"But Romeo does."

"Don't speak to me of that nincompoop. I rue the day I ever met him. I knew when I first laid eyes on him he was a moonling. You must try to forgive me for ever suggesting you have anything to do with him, Belle. He isn't fit for human company. He ought to be locked up."

"Wrestling is really very civilized," Belle said apologetically. "I mean it's better than shooting your opponent, and killing him. It is the way matters were settled in old Greece."

"And what have nanny goats and billy goats to do with *me*, I should like to know? Renfrew was laughing at me the whole time. I'm sure I heard a rumble in his voice."

Belle subsided into quiet regrets. "And to think, just this evening as we prepared for the party, we were congratulating ourselves on having attached such eligible *partis*. I wonder if Basil—"

Jane silenced her with a glare. "Pray don't use this little setback as an excuse to saddle your cousin with a penniless wife. You would not be doing Basil any favor to encourage him."

"But who can I marry, then?" Belle asked, and burst into noisy tears.

Who indeed? "She's all yours." The words played in Jane's mind, raising her anger to a higher pitch at every repetition. He had only done it to make her look more attractive to that fool of a Romeo. That's what he thought of her, that she would make a stern keeper for the Grecian oddity. Renfrew had often said he wanted to keep Romeo in England, and obviously he was too dangerous to be on the loose alone. That was what future he had designed for her. A guardian for a lunatic, while he chased after loose women. And she had been fool enough to mistake that for love.

At Nicolson's, Renfrew quietly closed the library door and sat with his head in his hands, reliving the worst five minutes of his life. He had never felt like such a fool, and worse, a scoundrel. Jane was right. He had been planning a wretched future for her. What right had he to interfere in her life? He had unwittingly given her hopes of attaching himself—an unconscionable thing to have done. He shouldn't have been so much with her. It was only natural that some closeness should develop. He had become very fond of her, too, fond enough that he was already beginning to dislike the thought of her marrying Romeo. Oh, dear— Romeo. He'd take this news hard. Worse, it wouldn't dampen his ardor one iota. He expected Athene to have a vile temper.

Which she certainly had. He had never seen such fire in a lady's eyes before. A reluctant smile tugged at his lips. Jane obviously wasn't the sort of lady to go into a decline. A fighter—he liked that. There was a good deal he liked about Jane Halsey. A pity he had been banned from ever seeing her again. He'd have to write a note and apologize, and that would be the end of this Season's infatuation.

Chapter Seven

"SO YOU'VE finely done it," Miss Munch declared, in high dudgeon, when she heard the story. "I knew it was too good to last. A pair of duke's sons, and what must you do but give them a taste of your tongue." It was Miss Halsey who received the first blaze of her wrath, and even that blast was soon deflected toward the gentlemen. "Not that they didn't deserve it, I'm sure. Trying to stick you with a moonling. You're well out of it all, girls. There's better onions in the stew than ever came out of it."

Munch had a heart as soft as cotton wool where her girls were concerned. A Jane with her face set in a permanent mask of frozen indifference was almost worse than a Belle in tears, as she so often was over the next few days. There were periods of dry eyes, of course. The message from Renfrew received the next morning revived her spirits, till Jane chucked it into the grate unopened. After

Belle had retrieved it and read it, her eyes moistened again.

"It only says he is sorry if he caused us any inconvenience."

"Nothing about coming to call?" Miss Munch demanded, and Jane, too, listened with sharp ears.

"He says he will respect Miss Halsey's request not to call on her."

"Request! It was an order!" Jane exclaimed, and tore the note from Belle's fingers to chuck it back into the grate.

Mrs. Pettigrew was disappointed with the termination of the romance, too. "Pity," she said, shaking her capped head. "Just the sort of people who could have done any amount of good for Basil's career. You do not think you could come to care for Lord Romeo?" she asked hopefully.

"Never as a husband," Jane said firmly, and was required to repeat her decision several times over the next days. No enumeration of his wealth, his noble birth, and distinguished connections could budge her an inch.

There was another interruption in Belle's tears when word was sent abovestairs of Romeo's arrival in the saloon the next afternoon.

"Tell him I am out," Jane said firmly.

"I'll see him!" Belle exclaimed.

"He didn't ask to see you," Munch told her.

"Do you mind, Jane?" Belle asked.

Jane sat on the bed and opened a fashion magazine. "Suit yourself."

There was a flurry of drying Belle's eyes, brushing her hair, tidying her toilette, and making the fearful descent into the saloon. Mrs. Pettigrew was out visiting friends, and as Jane stuck to her resolve to also be out, it fell to Miss Munch to play propriety. For this signal occasion, she removed her apron and added her one note of elegance, a carved ivory brooch, to her gown. Thus far, she had seen only the top of Romeo's head as he entered and left the house, and his boots over the banister when he was in the front hall. She was bowled over by the exquisite dandy, and said not a word from head to toe of his visit. "My breath fair flew out my ears" was how she later described her reaction to Miss Halsey. "He looks just like the angels in my prayer-book."

The meeting was brief. "I want to see Athene," Romeo announced.

"She's out," Belle replied.

"When she will be back?"

"She won't. That is—she doesn't want to see you, Romeo."

Romeo frowned at the floor. "This requires cogitation. You'll be hearing from me again. Pray remind your sister that whatever she may have overheard in the garden, she could not have heard any disparagement from *my* lips, for none has ever been uttered."

"I'll tell her," Belle said.

He rose and left the house, muttering, "Lovers' quarrels are the renewal of love."

But as soon as he was beyond the door, love yielded to business, and he was off to search out a captain for the excellent ship he had hired. So clever of his cousin Damien to arrange for hiring one. It was much cheaper than having to buy an entire vessel, when he only required it for a few weeks. Damien Carruthers was that practical sort of gentleman who knew things, like James. He could bother to carry in his head, for instance, that the Battle of Waterloo had been fought between

June fifteenth and eighteenth. He even knew who had won it. He knew also that the new stone bridge honoring the battle was to open on the anniversary of that victory. And what he did not know, Romeo thought with a sly smile, would not hurt him. Ah, but it would hurt Renfrew. His heart congealed at the very thought of his perfidious brother.

It was half an hour before he was able to think clearly again. And again, he thought of Damien Carruthers. There was the fellow to find him a captain. A brief stop at the East India Company put him in touch with Cousin Damien. The next stop was Burlington House, to continue the search for Thalia's head, and to befriend the herb—what was it again?—Basil. Basil . . . he must remember that. People were strangely attached to their dreadful English names. Miss Quinn had taken it quite amiss when he called her Miss Squint. This mnemonics was a tricky business: Miss Squint had seemed so excellent an aid, as the lady even had a strangely narrowed eye.

During this short period, life was hardly more pleasant at Stapford House than on Catherine Street. Renfrew thought often of that awful evening at the Nicolsons' rout. It was all his fault. He had sicced Romeo on Jane, had encouraged and abetted him every step of the way. He was guilty of that, and not innocent of Romeo's charge either. He *had* flirted with Jane. He had let her love him. He knew she was falling in love with him, and had done nothing to discourage her. He had taken it quite as his due. Women were always falling in love with him, and he with them. Love was supposed to be a game, fun—and not this awful heaviness of guilt and remorse.

Jane despised him. How could she not? He despised himself. He was a thoroughly despicable person, and a thoroughly miserable one. How perverse of fate to have pitched him into love with the one woman in London who hated him. And the final indignity was that rather than having grown closer to his brother by the whole wretched affair, Romeo had turned on him, too. Naturally he had had to tell Romeo that Jane had overheard their discussion. "You think to run the country, James, and you can't even handle a simple love affair," he had said. Words had led to words, and soon to a total breakdown between them.

Lord Romeo was teaching his mama a lesson by not speaking to her directly, and as he no longer conversed with his brother either, he was mute, except for an occasional command to a servant. But then he was seldom at home. Just what he was doing, no one knew. Renfrew suspected he had patched it up with Jane and was passing his afternoons and evening with the Halseys. She would marry Romeo to spite him. He conscientiously told himself this was entirely Miss Halsey's affair. He would be happy if Jane had decided to accept Romeo's offer. She would make an unexceptionable sister-in-law, so long as he never had to see her. To see her and not touch her would be hell. To touch her and not declare his love would be impossible. So when the marriage occurred, he must not interfere if Romeo suggested spiriting his bride off to Greece. He knew Romeo had sold some stocks, which suggested he was accumulating money to return there, and told himself this was for the best.

To add to his troubles, the duchess had become as snappish as a hungry dog. As Renfrew believed Romeo was courting Jane, there was no point burdening Mama with details of the quarrel. She was bad-humored enough without that. The Season was over, and why must she remain in horrid London when her roses were in bloom? "I thought the Halseys were to come to tea," she said from time to time. "I will not give my permission to marriage with a lady we have never even met! Why does she not come? The truth now, James: is she not fit to be seen in public?"

"She's fine, Mama. A very—nice girl." The loveliest girl in London, with stormy gray eyes that turned jet black when she was angry. Her hair was glossy black, like a crow's wing, and tumbled in unruly curls around her ivory brow in the wind. . . .

"I don't call Catherine Street a nice address, not by a long shot. I think you could do better for your brother."

Romeo strolled into the room and looked about blandly, as though the gold saloon were empty. He rang the bell and asked the servant to pour him a glass of wine, "And if you will be so kind, pray tell the duchess I will not be home for dinner."

"Pray tell Lord Romeo if he comes in after midnight, I would be grateful if he did not start that hammering in his father's study," Her Grace retorted.

"You may tell Her Grace that the mantel in Papa's study is finished—but for a lick of paint. As to the rest of this obscene domicile, it must remain as it is. Barbarians, apparently, find it satisfactory." Romeo drank his wine, gave a shudder of revulsion at a fine Stubbs painting on the wall, and left.

"Why is he behaving this way?" the exasperated mother demanded of her sane son.

"He is angry with me."

"That much is obvious. Why is he angry?"

Renfrew subdued a guilty flush and hunched his shoulders. "You know Romeo."

"That I do not. I never knew him. I have come to believe the boy is a changeling."

For a week, the affair of Romeo and Renfrew loomed large on Catherine Street. But as day followed day and the gentlemen failed to appear after Romeo's one visit, they were spoken of less. It was clear from Jane's wan cheeks and lackluster manner that she still regretted her missed chance, but Belle began to revive. She discovered the pleasures of gothic novels, and was making herself a new sprigged muslin gown. Mrs. Pettigrew eyed it askance and suggested it might be a good idea for Munch to remove the girls' gowns to their own room as she was finding her closet a trifle crowded.

Strangely enough it was Basil who reintroduced the name Lord Romeo into the house. It occurred over dinner one evening, when his Mama made a query as to how affairs were progressing at Burlington House. "I really ought to drop around and see the Elgin Marbles," she finished.

"You have left it too late, Mama. They're all packed up for the big move to the museum. You will have to wait and see them after they are arranged there."

"Did you find Thalia's head?" Belle asked.

"Yes, as a matter of fact, we did. Lord Romeo has been a wonderful help. I'm ashamed to say he knows a deal more about the Marbles than I do. He often spends a few hours there, picking about the debris, you know. He has pieced a bit of frieze together for us beautifully. In fact, he is so helpful, he has been given his own key, and comes and goes like a regular employee, except of course he will not accept any pay for his work. I daresay he wants to see his fill of the Marbles before he leaves the country."

"Leaves the country!" Belle gasped.

"Why, yes, he plans to return to Greece soon. Did you not know?"

Belle tossed her curls in Jane's direction. "How should *we* know anything about him? He never comes here anymore. Will he be going alone?"

"I shouldn't think so. The ship he's hired would hold half of London. A regular frigate. Some connection of his managed to hire him an EIC ship that was standing idle for a few months."

"I mean will he be taking a bride with him?" Belle explained.

"He hasn't said so. I did hear from one of his servants, though, that he is having a deal of work done to the vessel, so perhaps he's fixing it up to suit a lady. That will be a novel honeymoon for her."

"It is fine to be on terms with Lord Romeo, but you ought not to be too chummy with his servants, Basil," his mother mentioned.

"They are practically my servants, too, Mama. Lord Romeo often brings two or three men with him, to help haul the heavy marbles about. They are better trained and more careful than the louts the museum has been able to get hold of."

"Perhaps I will go and see the Marbles again tomorrow," Belle said with a sly smile.

"I already told Mama, they're not on exhibit now," Basil reminded her.

"There must be other things to see at Burlington House."

"There is a painting in the office next door that always reminds me of Halsey Hall," Basil mentioned. "The setting is quite like it, but if it is your old home, there was once a portico out front. You would probably know for certain."

"I can't imagine what it would be doing at Burlington House," Mrs. Pettigrew said. "The Halseys are no kin to the Boyles. Perhaps someone on Lady Burlington's side of the family—but I have no idea what her maiden name was." This conversation petered out for lack of knowledge and interest.

It was not Lord Romeo's connection with Basil that precipitated the next step in the affair. It was the very impatient Duchess of Stapford. She would wait no longer to go to her roses, but to appease her conscience, she determined to visit the Halseys, and see if the girl would do for Romeo. She realized there was some difficulty in the romance, and feared Miss Halsey was unfit to be presented, which would not deter Romeo one whit. If a notice should suddenly reach Hampshire of the wedding, she wished to know what she should tell her husband about the bride. It seemed unlikely Renfrew would countenance any ineligible connection, but he was behaving oddly, too. He had discovered something to Miss Halsey's discredit, and was trying to keep it from her.

On a warm afternoon in mid-June she donned her blue pelisse and a very plain bonnet and had the carriage called. Within minutes, she landed at Catherine Street, where her arrival threw the entire household into turmoil. Jane could ignore a summons from Lord Romeo, but when a white card bearing the duchess's name was handed to her by a speechless Munch, she fell into uncertainty. To decline a summons from such a prestigious lady seemed impossible. Her breeding demanded a polite reply, and she nodded to Munch.

"I shall be down presently. Pray offer Her Grace a glass of wine, and see that she is comfortable."

"She is comfortable. The mistress took her out to the backyard to see the rosebush. The duchess spotted it through a chink in the fence. That'll give you time to tidy up," Munch said.

Even such a lover of the rose as the duchess could not spend more than five minutes admiring one straggly specimen of an undistinguished strain. When Jane and Belle entered the saloon, the duchess was already ensconced with a glass of wine, which she found surprisingly good for such a modest household. Her decisions had already been made. James was right, as she ought to have known. The family was well-bred, but had fallen on hard financial times. Miss Halsey was just the sort of lady that would do for Romeo.

Both girls curtsied very daintily, and expressed the proper degree of welcome. Obviously well-bred, but not so sophisticated that they could conceal their curiosity regarding her call.

"I have been meaning to drop in forever," the duchess said vaguely. "James once promised to bring you for tea, ladies, but he has been so busy at the house, I took matters into my own hands, as it were."

"How very thoughtful of you to call," Miss Jane Halsey said, with still that questioning light in her stormy eyes.

Odd that James should speak of the younger chit's beauty. This one was more in his style. He always had a sweet tooth for those raven-haired gels.

Mrs. Pettigrew took up the conversational strain. "We heard Lord Romeo is also very busy, lending a hand with the move of the Elgin Marbles to the British Museum."

"Ah, is that what he is up to? He isn't speaking to me these days, you must know. Well, that should keep him out of mischief."

The ladies exchanged a surprised look, and discussed Basil's work with the museum. The duchess accepted another glass of wine, and scanned the table for a biscuit to accompany it. Jane bit back any questions that occurred to her regarding how James was occupying himself. A little later Belle mentioned that Romeo had hired a ship.

"Hired a frigate?" the duchess demanded, dumbfounded. "What the devil for?"

"Why, for his return to Greece," Belle said.

"He would surely not require a frigate only to go to Greece. That would carry a whole army. No, no, you must have misunderstood, Miss Belle. You may be sure he has bought a yacht. Romeo loves yachting. So he is returning to Greece, then. Well, I cannot say I am surprised. He never has a good word to say about anything in England—except for a certain young lady," she added, with a questioning glance at Jane.

Jane met the look with such self-command that the duchess could learn nothing from it.

"A very cool customer" was how she described Miss Halsey to Renfrew that evening. "She will do excellently for Romeo."

"What did you think of Belle? She is usually deemed the prettier of the two."

"No, no, she is too soft. She is not Stapford material," she added, with a gimlet look to see if this had any effect on her eldest son. There was no fierce defense of the young lady, as there would have been if he fancied himself in love with the chit. "She could never manage Romeo, but Miss Halsey will do excellently. Where did you find such a treasure, James?"

"At Burlington House."

"What has set the pair at odds, Romeo and Miss Halsey? She did not respond at all to any little hints I let out regarding her accompanying him to Greece. I wonder if she is trying to talk him into staying in England."

As his mother was now in contact with the Halseys, Renfrew saw he would have to confess. "Perhaps the fault is partly mine, Mama. I had to spend some time with the Halseys, too, to steer Romeo straight. He took the notion I was interfering with his romance. There was a—slight contretemps at a rout party. The ladies have refused to see me since then."

His mother leapt on it like a dog on a bone. "Interfering in what way? Flirting with Miss Halsey, I warrant. I thought her very much in your style. So that is why Romeo is not speaking to you: he is jealous. But that couldn't be simpler to rectify, James. You have only to tell him she means nothing to you, to explain."

"I tried that. He doesn't believe me."

"If he won't believe words, he will believe actions. I had planned to return to Hampshire tomorrow, but I would so like to see Romeo safely in Miss Halsey's hands that I shall delay my departure a few days to bring them together. I shall have a party and invite the Halseys. Romeo is leaving soon for Greece, you know. He has bought a yacht. If we don't send him back safely shackled to an English lady, there is no saying who he will take up with. We must convince Miss Halsey to have him."

"And what action am I to perform to convince Romeo I'm not an ogre?"

"You are not to do anything, especially anything that would lead him to believe you are angling after his lady."

"Once he gets an idea into his pate—"

"Pooh! Did I give birth to *two* moonlings? You must bring the prettiest lady in London to the party, and dote on her all evening. If Miss Halsey had some notion of attaching you, that will show her she shoots too high. I daresay that is what is at the bottom of all this: Miss Halsey misunderstood your attentions. She thought she might have a chance with you, and that is why she discouraged Romeo, but when she sees how matters truly stand, she'll jump at the chance to get Romeo. Not a bad match for the daughter of a baronet—and her papa is dead to boot. The estate and title went to an uncle, I think you said?"

"Yes, so I understand."

"Excellent. The girl must feel she is living in a closet in that little house. And with one poor Queen Anne rose, reaching vainly for the sunlight in the backyard. It looked like an orphan. They planted the poor thing next the house, too, when anyone could have told them a rose needs sunlight. She will accept, certainly. It is up to you to show her your total indifference. That will turn the trick."

"Should we connive and trick the girl into having Romeo?"

His mother narrowed her eyes. "Finding him a strong wife was *your* suggestion. There was no talk of conniving and trickery then."

"But that was before—"

The duchess drew a deep, impatient breath. Really, sons were stupider than daughters, once they went imagining themselves in love. "Before you decided you had a fancy for her yourself?"

Renfrew was bursting to talk about his own problem. "I didn't mean for it to happen, Mama. Truly, I didn't want to— But she is so—"

"Fiddlesticks! She is fine enough for Romeo, but you can and shall do a deal better for yourself than an orphan of no more than respectable parentage. You know you fall in love every spring, James. Go and fall in love with some attractive lightskirt. Have an affair, and get over this stupid notion of loving Romeo's fiancée. You will be out of love before the leaves fall. We both know it. Let her marry Romeo and take him to Greece. She will be very busy there, stopping Romeo from squandering their money on temples and ruins. She will have a fine brood of children in no time, and be an excellent mother to them."

Renfrew clenched his lean jaws and glared. "No, she won't. She'll be cold and hard-hearted, like you."

"That is how excellent mothers must behave— firmly, or their idiot sons would marry all the wrong ladies."

"Romeo's right. You *are* heartless."

The duchess pulled the bell cord to summon a servant. "Pray tell Lord Renfrew his mother would appreciate it if he would draw up a short list of guests for an informal dinner and rout party on Friday. And send a card to Catherine Street first. If they refuse, you may throw the rest of the cards into the dustbin."

"Yes, milady."

There was no actual repetition of the messages in these three-way conversations. Renfrew pinched his nostrils and said to the servant, "Pray tell Her

Grace I shall be too busy to act as her secretary. If she plans to connive and trick her own son into marriage with the wrong lady, she may not count on my assistance. I shall be busy in Parliament Friday evening."

"You may tell Lord Renfrew I shall handle the invitations, and I shall expect him for dinner at seven-thirty on Friday. If he is not here, I shall send a gang of ruffians to forcibly remove him from the House." On this uncompromising speech, the duchess strode from the room.

The servant gave Renfrew a leery look. "She will, you know."

"Are all families as weird as this one, Huddleston, or are we exceptional?"

"All weird in their own way, Your Lordship. Old Lady Comstock, where my brother is in service, lives in the attics amid rubble for fear of harming her good furnishings downstairs. She sits all day in a broken armchair sipping tea from a cracked cup, and only goes below in her stocking feet each morning to see that all is in order."

"Good. I'm relieved to know we're not the biggest fools in the country."

"Oh, no, sir. There's plenty as foolish as your lot here."

A gleam of appreciation lit Renfrew's dark eye. "Quite. Could I bother you for just one more favor, Huddleston? Pray tell me to stop being such a jackass."

"Consider it said, Your Lordship."

Chapter Eight

*T*HE INVITATION to the rout party at Stapford House was duly received and threw the Halseys into another fit of indecision.

"What can it mean?" Jane asked. "How can we get out of it without offending Her Grace?"

Cards came for the entire household. Mrs. Pettigrew was by no means eager to refuse such a prestigious invitation. Quite apart from the pleasure it would give her, and the manifold benefits to Basil, it would provide her nieces with any number of new and eligible acquaintances.

"Get out of it?" she exclaimed. "I have no intention of declining the offer. Her Grace was most condescending. This could do not only Basil but you girls any amount of good. You cannot refuse, Jane!"

Belle added her entreaties. "Oh, do let us go. We have been as dull as ditch water since Renfrew and Romeo dropped us."

"They did not drop *us*! We dropped *them*."

"Well, Renfrew didn't call, and Romeo only came

once. I daresay he has found some other lady to pester by now. This is Renfrew's way of renewing the acquaintance without risking a direct rebuff."

Jane's heart rose insensibly at the idea, but she soon dampened its enthusiasm. She had made a fool of herself once by imagining love when there was none. Worse, she had revealed her feelings to Renfrew. At best, he perhaps wished to apologize, and she felt she had been more forceful in her outburst than she now liked. She would accept his apology, and admit she had overreacted. And if at all possible, she would convince him her anger had nothing whatsoever to do with his own uninterest in her.

"If you are all determined to attend, then I suppose I must bow to superior numbers," she agreed.

A reply was sent off with a speed that quite revived the duchess's spirits. No sooner was the acceptance safely in hand than she sent her footman off to deliver the other cards. That evening, she gave off speaking to Renfrew through the footman and told him directly, "They're coming."

This oblique statement was understood without any further elucidation. In his excitement, Renfrew answered before he realized he had done it. "All of them?" he demanded eagerly.

"All. The next item is to shanghai Romeo and make sure he is here."

"He'll be here."

"I'd like to have your confidence. What makes you think so?"

"I have heard no scandal of his annoying any other lady with his attentions, so he must still be after Jane."

"I daresay he is seeing her, or how would the Halseys have known he had bought that yacht.

Shall I send Romeo a card, or have the servants tell him?"

"I'll put a card with his other invitations, and hope he sends us a reply." The idiocy of this means of communicating with a member of his own household sent Renfrew off into chuckles.

"It is no laughing matter, James. I hate to think what the world would say if they had any notion how we go on here. There cannot be another family in all of England that is so difficult to manage."

"I expect they'd drop their cracked teacups in shock."

His mother frowned in forgivable confusion and ate her dinner.

It was past midnight when Lord Romeo entered Stapford House and took his pile of invitations to his room. He found it not peculiar that he received an invitation to his own house. In fact, he smiled rather fondly at it. Poor old James; he wished to mend the rift. Perhaps he would oblige him before leaving. This rout would be his farewell party, though the family did not know it. But there must be no rapprochement before the party. The constraint between them suited his present activities. It would not do to have James asking too many questions about how he filled his days, and spent his money, at this critical juncture.

Time really was running very short. In the crush of business, Athene had slid to the back of his mind, but he had not by any means forgotten her. A vision of her loveliness often came at night to trouble his rest. It was the lack of opportunity to visit a prostitute that caused it, very likely. Men had their needs. Perhaps Athene would be at the party? He would drop around to Catherine Street and visit the ladies tomorrow. Time heals all wounds, and by now she must be on thorns to see him again.

After having accepted the invitation, Jane thought it seemed rather foolish to turn Romeo from the door. As it happened, Jane and Belle were in the saloon when he arrived, and Jane agreed to let him be shown in. With luck, time might have worked some miracle, and he might fancy himself in love with Belle now. But when he rushed straight to Jane and crushed her two hands to his lips in a fever of bliss, she saw she was out in her reckoning.

"Don't be so foolish, Romeo. Have a seat and behave like a gentleman if you wish to remain," she said tartly.

He smiled one of his beatific smiles and drew a chair close to hers, while Belle sat on, unnoticed. All his former admiration of Athene was rekindled at a glance. She was even more admirable than he remembered. He saw her standing at the helm of his frigate with him, eyes straining for the first sight of Greece, while the zephyrs riffled her curls. "A man must have his faults, as wise Petronius tells us. If Athene decrees foolishness is mine, so be it. Who would dare to contradict the goddess of wisdom? Are you impatient with me for neglecting you, Athene?"

"Not at all."

"A truly noble forbearance."

Her temper piqued at his obtuseness, she added, "In fact, I am grateful."

"You do me too much honor. You think I have been forcibly restraining myself from coming to you, but it is not the case. Love has yielded to business. My absence does not indicate any lessening of my love, however."

"Now don't start that!"

"They are not wise who buffet against love," he chided softly.

"Neither are they wise who imagine love where there is none."

After a moment's pause in the conversation, Belle asked, "What business is it you're involved in, Romeo? Is it the yacht you bought?"

"Yacht? I didn't buy a yacht. Who has been deceiving you?"

"Your mother told us you had."

"You have met Mama, then?"

"She came to call," Jane said, and looked for an explanation.

"How odd! This smells like James's work. He is trying to help me, to make up for past offenses. Next time you see her, pray tell her I have not bought a yacht."

"Have you not?" Belle asked. "Basil thought you were hiring a frigate, but of course that is ridiculous."

Both ladies looked for his reply. "I have engaged a ship," he said vaguely, "for my return home."

The day was splendid, and Jane decided it would be more amusing to go out for a drive than to sit inside. "Why don't you take us down to see the ship, Romeo?"

He appeared a little reluctant at first, but decided it was a hopeful sign that Jane was interested. "Yes, you will want to approve it before we leave, but if you have in mind to start buying curtains and things, I ought to warn you, time is short, my pet."

"Curtains?" She laughed.

He nodded. "I have earned your derision, and must accept it. What concern would Athene have in curtains? This very room is a testament to your lack of interest in things domestic." He cast a blighting eye over the fatigued appointments of the chamber.

"Thank you," she said through unsteady lips.

"Do we have to take your little sister with us?"

"Yes, we do," Jane said unequivocally, refusing to soften her reply with any explanation.

On this halfhearted sort of invitation, Belle went upstairs for their pelisses and bonnets. The carriage awaiting the ladies was not the straw basket but a proper city chaise, drawn by matched bays.

Romeo said in Jane's ear, "Next time I shall drive my curricle, to preclude bringing along a chaperon. We must be alone very soon, Athene. I cannot much longer be deprived of at least your lips."

A seducer who so guilelessly betrayed his ruses in advance could not be taken as much of a threat. A spontaneous laugh fell from Jane's lips, and Romeo dropped into a trance of admiration. They were driven to the docks, where the ladies were well-entertained looking at ships of all sizes and sorts. The busy bustle of loading and unloading vessels, the salt air alive with hollering voices, the sight of a few dusky foreigners in their native garb and several uniformed naval officers, made the trip worthwhile. The ladies nearly forgot why they had come, but Romeo called them to attention.

"I have the *Justice* anchored just along here," he said, leading them forward. "You won't mind boarding by means of a plank? It is quite safe, and if you fall in, I shall rescue you, even though I am wearing a new jacket. You have not complimented me on it, by the by."

"Very nice," Jane said.

Belle noticed that she might as well be at home, for all the attention Romeo paid to her. After half an hour, she began to find him more ridiculous, and less handsome than she remembered.

They soon stood looking at a ship that loomed as high in the sky as the dome of St. Paul's Cathedral. "Surely this cannot be the *Justice!*" Belle exclaimed. "It's so huge!"

"You noticed the lack of a name painted on the side. I have only rented her, you see. They call ships 'she'—perhaps because they *can* be rented," he added. "I regret the name is not blazoned in gold broadside, but then we look higher for justice, and if you will lift your eyes, you will see I have had a flag designed. The crudeness of the execution is a disappointment. The seamstress quite destroyed my elegant design."

They obediently lifted their gaze, and saw fluttering in the breeze an enormous red flag, with the symbol of justice done in gold. It was only the bust of the blindfolded woman, but she held aloft the scales. Romeo inclined his head to Jane and said softly, "When the flag is blown straight out, you will, perhaps, recognize the model I used for Justice. I regretted having to cover your sublime orbs, Athene. The symbolism, however, was necessary."

Jane bit back a smile at his foolishness, and said, "Justice is your own name for the ship, then?"

"Yes, the EIC, with the obsequiousness of philistine commercialism, called it the *Royal Charlotte.*"

"What is the symbolism of your name, Justice?"

A sly, secretive smile curved Romeo's lips. Such an expression looked out of place on his open face. He resembled a child, planning some innocent prank. He longed to reveal all to Athene, to warm his heart at the fire of her approval. But as well as being Pallas Athene, she was also Jane Halsey, and it was from this less important personage he must conceal his scheme. "It seemed a suitable virtue. You wouldn't want me to call her Injustice, would you?"

"No, indeed, though it seems to me there is some injustice in one man being able to hire such an enormous ship just to fan his vanity. Why didn't you buy a yacht? This frigate will be of no use to you in island-hopping, or whatever you plan to do once you reach Greece."

"I have only rented the ship. I have a large quantity of items to take back to Greece—my garden carriage, half a dozen horses. I have my own yacht anchored in the Gulf of Corinth."

"Well, shall we board her?"

"How quickly you have picked up the jargon. I daresay this is the first time you've ever *seen* a frigate, and already you speak as though you know what you're talking about."

"If that is a compliment, I thank you."

"Merely an observation."

He led the ladies up the plank and on to a ship that was far from luxurious. It seemed to be well enough maintained, but the living quarters, which were the only part the ladies were interested in, were small, sparsely furnished, and without one single luxury.

"We shall dine, of course, at the captain's table," he said, pointing to a table that would seat perhaps half a dozen. The table was laid with plain steel cutlery and heavy dishes. "My captain is a Mr. Holmes, retired from active naval service. An older gentleman, but game for one last bat—engagement. Do let me show you the sleeping quarters, ladies."

These, too, were minimal. Romeo eyed with a dissatisfied frown the pair of bunks in what was apparently his sleeping compartment. "They'll have to go. I'll buy a double bed."

Jane's lips twitched, and as she stole a glance at Belle, she noticed her sister, too, had overcome any slight tendresse for this peculiar gentleman. Her eyes danced with laughter.

"You will want a canopied bed, I suppose?" Belle asked impishly.

Romeo measured the door, and mentally measured his own canopied bed at home. "I shall have a carpenter build one in the room," he decided. "But it will have to be plain, I fear. There is not time for carving cupids and flowers. Voluminous hangings of velvet will remove the air of a dungeon."

"Well, one only sleeps in a bedroom after all. Let us see the saloon," Jane said.

"Sleeps?" Romeo asked, surprised. "Yes, that, too. I had forgotten. But once the first fever of love-making has abated, I daresay we will want to sleep as well. It is a fatiguing enough business."

The saloon was small, but neatly appointed with the essentials—sofas, chairs, tables, lamps, and a carpet on the floor. The minuscule windows were uncurtained. Polished brass twinkling in odd and unexpected places gave the room a nautical air. Romeo saw Athene was less than enchanted with the living arrangements, and urged her to make any improvements that occurred to her, provided they could be made quickly.

"Don't be ridiculous. I shan't be accompanying you. Fix it up to suit yourself."

"If it is my lack of mentioning marriage that deters you, naturally I would be willing to make it legal. Marriage is a slave institution. Love ought not to have to be legislated, and it is especially futile to make two half-mad people vow to love each other forever, when experience has proved the temporary nature of love. But there are legal points to consider, of course. I would not want the fruits of our union to be illegal. Mama, I daresay, would dislike it."

"I trust you haven't been picking up a special license behind my back?" Jane asked.

"Why, no, I confess that slipped my mind. I am not sure it is necessary for a shipboard wedding, performed by the captain. I wonder if Captain Holmes has his prayer book on board."

They soon left, and went for a drive in the park. "Will you be attending your mother's rout party, Romeo?" Belle asked.

"Certainly. It is my farewell party, you know."

"When, exactly, will you be leaving?"

"The weather will have something to say about that, but soon after the party. One dislikes to linger after farewells have been said. I say, Herbert will be attending the party, too, I trust?"

"Yes, he and his mother are attending," Jane replied.

"Good!"

"And his name is still Basil, incidentally."

"He has asked me to call him Herbert. The study of mnemonics proved a disaster. Between calling Lady Lieven 'Lady Dead,' and Lady Jersey 'Lady Guernsey,' I have fallen into odium, and abandoned it."

The ladies exchanged a laughing eye, and Jane said, "That might be best."

She wanted to make an inquiry about Renfrew,

particularly whether he would be attending the rout, but disliked to ask. After a private word with her sister, Belle posed the question for her.

"I have no reason to believe he will not be present. Naturally I have not spoken to him about it—"

Jane was overcome with a sudden fear that he had left town, or something had happened to him. "Why not?" she asked.

"We are not on speaking terms, after his heinous conduct at that rout party. I took him to account. He denied the whole, but not with the vigor of truth. James never can resist flirting with a pretty woman. It is something in the blood, I suppose. I am similarly afflicted."

"Why are you not speaking to him, then, if you understand his weakness?" Jane asked. Her voice was hard. "Flirting with a pretty woman"—that's all it had been.

"I saw the look on his face when he was dancing with you, Athene. And on yours, too."

Belle chose that tense moment to air her views. "Jane has told you she has no intention of marrying you, Romeo. I think it is unfair of you to interfere between her and Lord Renfrew."

"I only charged him with the crime. He's a free agent. If he loved Jane, he would not be deterred by a little competition. Quite the contrary. Am I correct in concluding he has not been seeing you?" he asked Jane.

"Quite correct. I haven't seen him since that evening."

"Then you know who is the truer lover. I daresay James has another lady on the string by now, but I have been continent. In all truth I must own it is the crush of business more than fidelity to you that accounts for it, but—"

Jane's temper simmered to hear Renfrew was engaged with another lady. Before she spoke, Belle exclaimed, "Oh, look! There is the Prince Regent! How well he sits his mount."

Romeo looked and shook his head. "I detest to see cruelty to animals. Someone ought to inform the Prince it is time he hired an elephant. Only look how that poor mare's back sags under the weight."

When he began rolling down the window to speak to the Prince, Jane grabbed his hand, and he was easily diverted to fighting to keep it.

Chapter Nine

LORD RENFREW was pleasantly surprised to receive a formal call from his brother in his office that evening. The pleasure diminished the instant Romeo opened his mouth.

"This is purely a business visit, James. In fact, I shall address you henceforth as Lord Renfrew, if I can remember. I want some of my money. It is humiliating that Papa has left you in charge of my funds, as though I were a child."

"You took out a few thousand just last week. Why do you need so much blunt?"

"Because I am returning to Greece very soon, and—"

"That was the excuse last week."

"It is not an excuse! It is the reason. If you must know, I have hired a ship, and had to pay the rent and seamen and supplies. Did you know an able-bodied seaman makes more than our vicar at home, James? Pardon me! I mean Lord Renfrew."

"That bit of knowledge had not come my way.

Since hiring a ship is so expensive, why don't you just book passage in the usual way?"

A soft smile lit Romeo's blue eyes. "This is to be no ordinary voyage, James. I'm sorry, I can't go on calling you Lord Renfrew. It sounds too silly. And I am too happy. It is to be my honeymoon."

Renfrew stiffened and his face turned noticeably pale. His blue eyes looked darker when he spoke, and his voice was chilly. "Am I to assume, then, that Miss Halsey has accepted your offer?"

"Yes, I am marrying her on board the ship," he said, and looked closely at James for his reaction. "You haven't heard?"

"No, I haven't seen her since—since the night of Nicolson's rout."

"Ah." Romeo smiled in satisfaction. This made his story much easier, though he would stick to the truth as much as possible. "We have decided a shipboard wedding would be romantic. Jane had no objection."

"I see. I trust the ceremony will be performed *before* the ship leaves the dock, for the sake of your bride's reputation."

"Yes, yes, don't worry your head about the details. Oh, there is just one thing—I shan't require a special license, shall I? Jane mentioned it . . ."

"I have no idea."

"Now, that is odd, James. You always know everything. Is it reluctance to assist me that makes you suddenly ignorant, I wonder?"

"You have overestimated the extent of my knowledge. I simply don't know, but it cannot be difficult to find out. Ask a bishop—or your captain."

"No matter. It is really the money I am come about."

"How much?"

"All of it—the funds, the Essex estate, everything except my Hampshire estate. I may possibly turn maudlin in my dotage, and wish to die in England. God knows the country is no good for living in, but it seems a fitting place to die."

James rapidly reviewed his brother's holdings, and felt a compelling reluctance to turn so much money over to this capricious youngster. Lord Romeo, though a younger son, was very rich.

"Why don't I just sell up the remainder of your consuls, and keep the rest invested? You can't possibly need all your money."

Romeo, too, did his arithmetic, and knew he would need more than a few thousand. It was the guns and mercenaries that had proved so expensive. He hoped they would not be necessary, but had to take every precaution. "I plan to purchase a small estate in Greece. We shall be living there," he answered blandly.

"You and Miss Halsey have discussed all this, have you?"

"Of course," he replied impatiently.

"Now, that is odd. When Mama was speaking to her, Miss Halsey said nothing of this shipboard wedding, or going to Greece. What is the big secret?"

"I didn't wish to upset Mama."

"She approves of the young lady. She would be very happy to see you marry and settle down. Did you ask Miss Halsey to keep it a secret?"

"No, but perhaps she thought Mama would dislike it. As she does not, what is the problem with giving me my money?"

Renfrew pondered it, and soon realized the only problem was his own unwillingness to smooth the lovers' path. "There is no problem. You and your bride pick out the property you want in Greece, and let me know the cost. I'll sell your shares and forward the money to you."

"Damme, James. I need it *now*. You've no idea how expensive everything is. My purse is empty. I need money. Just today I paid out a thousand pounds in seamen's wages for the trip."

"A thousand pounds! Good God, how many men did you hire?"

"It takes a couple of dozen to run the ship."

"You must be traveling in high style. You're not poor, Romeo, but you're not a prince either."

Romeo put his head back and emitted a languorous sigh. "It's our honeymoon, James. I want everything to be especially nice."

"Miss Halsey doesn't strike me as a demanding lady."

"You wouldn't say so if you'd heard her disparaging everything. She wants a canopied bed built into the cabin, with velvet hangings. She didn't mention it, but I noticed her eyeing the table askance. The tableware was very simple."

James's brows drew together in a fleeting frown. That didn't sound like Jane. "Don't even think it," Romeo said. "She is not marrying me for the pleasure of spending my money. If that were her aim, she would have dangled after you."

But in fact, she *had* dangled after him. He hadn't imagined her warm smiles, her inviting glances, and her comments at various parties, which had almost assumed she was his partner. Had he imagined he saw love gleaming in those stormy gray eyes? Apparently so, if she had already acceded to Romeo's pleadings. She couldn't love Romeo. No sane woman could. It was cream-pot love. It was, in fact, exactly the sort of marriage he had sat down with his mother and plotted for Romeo, and he was furious at his own success. His spine stiffened at the knowledge, and when he spoke, his voice had a tinge of astringency.

"Whatever her motive in accepting your offer, and one assumes, of course, that it is esteem—"

"*Love*, James. You avoid the word as though it were an excrescence."

"Esteem," he continued blandly, "I cannot in good conscience watch you squander the better part of your patrimony on a honeymoon. I'll advance you another thousand. That must do. After you've chosen your house in Greece, I'll arrange further funds."

Romeo sat silent a moment, trying to invent further inducements, but he was not a professional liar after all, and his inventiveness ran dry. He would have to ask the mercenaries to accept half their pay in IOUs. His reputation was good.

"Oh, very well, but get me as much cash as you can. I want to buy a few personal things before I leave. Do you think, James, a diamond ring for Jane, or would ruby better suit her forceful style?"

"That is for you to discuss with the bride. It has nothing to do with me," James said brusquely, and pulled a paper forward to indicate he was busy.

"I daresay you want me to leave you alone. I recognize that not very subtle shifting of papers, just like Papa. Oh, but before I leave, did Mama send you an invitation to her rout party? Belle particularly inquired whether you would be attending. Actually Jane put her up to it. They were whispering together before Belle posed the question."

Renfrew felt a quickening of his pulse. Now, why did Jane want to know that, in particular? Did she want to gloat over him? To show her power with

Romeo? She knew it was his hope to keep Romeo in England.

"I'll be there. Tell me, Romeo, was it Miss Halsey's idea that you return to Greece immediately?"

Romeo shook his head. "It is for the husband to decree, and his mate to agree. Jane will do as I tell her. She wields some power over me now, but once I have had my way with her, she will find me a touch less compliant."

This speech set Renfrew's back up even higher than before. His voice was thin when he said, "It might be more discreet for you to keep silent on such home truths, Romeo."

"Do you know, James, I cannot figure out whether you love Jane, or hate her. I thought I smelled jealousy earlier, but now—do you have *any* feelings for her at all?"

"I respect her intelligence."

"Respect—that is not emotion. It is purely cerebral. Imagine your not knowing the difference! You only know facts, like a shopkeeper or mathematician, and here I have been thinking you were wise." Romeo rose daintily. "I shall see you at the rout on Friday, if not before. If you are wondering whether you ought to give me a wedding gift—not that I mean to suggest you should—I would prefer money. You may tell Mama the same, if you happen to be speaking to her. Good night, James."

Renfrew watched as his dapper little brother sauntered from the room, shaking his blond curls at various appointments that met with his disapproval as he went.

So Jane was marrying him. A sense of dreary depression settled like a pall around his heart. The only good in the arrangement was that the pair would be leaving for Greece, even before the wedding. Quite apart from losing Jane himself, many aspects of this hasty wedding troubled Renfrew. There was the inordinate amount of money required for the honeymoon. He really must look into this ship Romeo had hired, and see what nonsense the boy was up to. If he had hired a band and dancing girls, the thing must be undone. The shipboard wedding, too, seemed very vague. What if a captain required a license, and none had been obtained? Where would that leave Miss Halsey? Compromised, and with no certainty that Romeo would honor his obligation. The dreadful thought even occurred that Romeo had no intention of marrying her. He had heard a whiff of rumor that Romeo had tried his hand at abducting Lady Barbara Manfred, before her engagement to Lord Clivedon.

Renfrew met Clivedon at Whitehall the next morning and mentioned his fears. Clivedon's remarks threw him into a pelter of uncertainty.

"I know he's your own brother, Renfrew, but between the two of us, the boy is mad as a hatter. He *did* kidnap Babe, but she rescued herself. He mentioned something about the Rape of the Sabine Women. I wonder if he plans to carry off a whole crew of ladies this time. Why else has he hired an Indiaman?"

"What?"

"Oh, yes. He's hired a large EIC frigate, and is flying a homemade flag of some sort. I've heard there's a blindfolded lady on it. That gives one pause. Does it mean he's hoodwinking someone? Queer twists in the lad. I don't say there's any vice in him; he just thinks differently from the rest of humanity. It is his long sojourn in Greece that has twisted his mind. I wouldn't put it a pace past him to hoodwink Miss Halsey into sailing off to Greece with him, without the legal sanctions. Perhaps you ought to look into it. You don't want a scandal in the family."

"Perhaps I shall," Renfrew said weakly, and sent off for his carriage.

Wherever Romeo spent his days, it was certainly not at home. There was no point going there. The docks seemed a likely spot, but Catherine Street beckoned. Whether Romeo was there or not, it was necessary to speak to Miss Halsey, and determine whether she was victim or coconspirator in this strange business.

When Renfrew's carriage was recognized through the window, Jane turned into a statue, just before she was galvanized into motion. She jumped from her chair and said "What can he want?" to her sister.

Belle peered through the curtains. She saw the frown on Renfrew's face, and observed the speed of his advance. "He looks angry," she said.

"He's angry that we accepted the invitation to his mother's rout. That's what it is. He's come to tell us we can't attend."

"She wouldn't invite us if she didn't want us to come. She came here uninvited as far as that goes," Belle pointed out.

Within thirty seconds, Renfrew was shown into the room. His frowns had dissipated, and he wore a forced smile of civility.

"Ladies, I am happy I found you at home." At once his eyes turned to Jane. She looked slightly frightened, and very lovely, though there was a tinge of anger in her stormy eyes. It was impossible to imagine that this green girl was plotting some dire revenge on him. "I would like to speak to you in private, Miss Halsey. Would you excuse us, Miss Belle?"

"Oh, certainly."

Jane was thrown into confusion. She also felt a spark of annoyance at Renfrew's high-handed manner. "I have no secrets from my sister," she said, but Belle was already on her way out the door, and she made no further effort to detain her, but only offered Renfrew a seat. He sat on the very edge of his chair. She sensed an air of tension in his uncomfortable pose, and felt the gleam in his dark eyes. "What is it?" she demanded fearfully.

"That is for you to tell me, Miss Halsey. I am extremely curious about this marriage you and Romeo are about to embark on. Why the secrecy?"

Jane's face went blank. "Marriage? I am not marrying him!"

Renfrew stared, aware of the fierce pumping of his heart in joyful relief. "Not marrying him! But he's hired the honeymoon ship."

"Not for my benefit."

"And the house in Greece?"

Jane blinked in obvious astonishment. "I don't know what you are talking about."

"By God, he's pulled the wool over my eyes. If not you, then who? He's marrying someone. . . ." Or worse, he was planning to kidnap some hapless lady. Clivedon's words came back to trouble him. "Perhaps I'll find him down at the shipyards. I hear he's flying a strange flag of some woman with a bandage over her eyes."

"Justice—the flag represents Justice," Jane said. A quick flash of suspicion flared in Renfrew's breast. "Have you seen it?"

"Yes, Romeo took Belle and me down to the dock yesterday. It's the first time I've seen him since—

for a week," she said, with a flush of confusion at the memories of that dreadful evening. "He dropped in quite unexpectedly. He's hired a huge frigate, Renfrew. So strange . . . He did speak of marriage, but I assure you I did not agree to it."

"Little difference that would make to him. Take care or you'll find yourself shanghaied and carried off to Greece."

Jane gave a shiver of fearful excitement at the possibility. "Surely you're joking!"

"I wish I were. It was pretty well covered up, but Romeo has tried something of the sort before. The only bright spot is that he would have very little hope of success. The last time he tried it, the lady overpowered him, I understand."

"But it would be more difficult to escape from a ship. I can't even swim."

"Very likely that's why he's switched from dry land to water. I must go and have a look at this frigate. Could you tell me exactly where it's anchored." He gave a small, tentative smile. "Or come with me, and show me?"

Jane felt a heaving surge of excitement, but spoke primly. "Perhaps that would be easiest. I'll just get my bonnet and pelisse."

She darted upstairs where Belle was all ears to hear what had transpired. Her sister told her the gist of it while she dressed.

"And he wants you to go to the docks with him?" Belle smiled. "Oh, Jane, it looks as though—"

"Don't be foolish. It is just to save time in finding the ship."

Certainly the young lady wasted no time in flying downstairs.

Miss Munch crossed her arms and shook her head. "I hope she knows what she is about. Who's to say Lord Renfrew ain't delivering her straight into the hands of his crazy brother? They'll spirit her across the water into grease." It was as a smear of grease that Miss Munch envisaged the faraway island.

"Renfrew is quite sane."

"Hah. And blood is thicker than water, missie."

Chapter Ten

*T*HE EXIGENCY of their errand provided Jane and Renfrew a safe subject of conversation during the short trip to the docks, and removed the constraint that normally prevails during the first meeting after a violent argument. The air was tense, but there was no talk of misunderstandings or apologies, or any verbal indication that words had been exchanged. They spoke of Lord Romeo and his ship.

The ship was easy to spot, with its bright banner fluttering in the breeze. Even with its sails furled, it was an impressive sight. There was considerable activity on and about the vessel. It looked like a whole army of workmen were engaged there, one half removing items, the other half putting them on board. What was going aboard, though hidden under tarpaulins, was easy to guess at. A long voyage obviously required food and water, clean linen, and all manner of supplies. But what was under those tarpaulins the men walking down the gangplank to shore carried? Renfrew stepped forward and asked one of them. The man was stocky, broad-shouldered, with arms like ham hocks.

"We're clearing the hold, governor," the man replied cheerily.

"Clearing it of what?"

The man blinked and frowned. "Of what's in it," he said.

"Ah." Renfrew disliked to admit ignorance in front of Jane and said vaguely, "A bit of house-keeping, prior to the trip. Shall we go aboard?"

When the gangplank was clear, he took her elbow and led her up to the deck. Jane felt his touch like a brand through her sleeve. Before they had taken two steps, they were approached by an elderly, dark-visaged man, dressed like a gentleman, and carrying a heavy air of authority.

"I'm afraid I'll have to ask you to leave, sir," the man said brusquely. "This is a private ship. There's no one aboard but workers. We're not allowing visitors at this time."

"I'm Renfrew, Lord Romeo's brother, and this is his—fiancée, Miss Halsey." He presented her in this manner to insure admission to the ship.

"Captain Holmes," the man said, and offered his hand. He had not been present during Jane's tour, but had heard of it. He had cautioned the lad against bringing a lady on such a perilous journey. As he spoke his manner became less brusque, but an air of wariness had descended on him.

Jane had told Renfrew what she knew of Holmes's background, that he was a retired naval officer, and Renfrew made a mention of this. Holmes nodded and smiled, and said, "Your brother is not here at the moment, sir. I'll tell him you dropped by."

"I didn't come to see my brother, but to have a look around the ship."

There was objection written on every line of the captain's face, yet he sensed authority in Lord Renfrew. Before he found polite words for his refusal, Jane said, "I didn't see you here yesterday when Lord Romeo brought me to tour the *Justice*. He won't mind if I show Lord Renfrew around. You must see the saloon, Renfrew."

So saying, she took Renfrew's elbow and led him forth. The captain was at their heels, trying to stop them. "Everything is in a great mess, ma'am. 'Twould be better if you came back another time, when we're all shipshape."

"That's quite all right," Renfrew said, and walked off with Jane.

Holmes barked an order to a crewman, who darted down below to execute the command. Renfrew suspected the order was to conceal whatever was going forth. The captain dogged the couple's every step, and beguiled them with explanations of everything, showing how furnishings were either bolted down or heavy enough to withstand the heaving of heavy waters.

"Oh, you've no idea the bucking and heaving that goes on when the wind is up. Mind you, the sail to Greece is not so treacherous as some trips I've taken. The voyage to America, now, there is a dangerous crossing."

It was soon obvious to Renfrew that the captain had no intention of leaving them alone. As Lord Romeo's brother, he could hardly be suspected of sabotage, yet Holmes was at their heels like a shadow. There did not appear to be any inordinately lavish renovations going forth, so what was the secret?

"Your men tell me you're clearing the hold," Renfrew said, smiling in a friendly way. "I should have thought that would have been done when the ship landed."

"This old frigate's been standing idle a year. She was used as a storage bin for John Company," he said.

"Storing what?"

"Lumber. When one of the other ships was re-done, they put the old lumber in the hold here, till they decided what to do with it. Your brother didn't want the hold weighted down; it would slow the voyage."

"Surely ballast is required, to steady the ship in heavy water?" Renfrew asked. He was on uncertain ground, but persisted as best he could.

A blaze of frustration flared on Holmes's swarthy face. "We have our own supplies to carry, sir. You must know Lord Romeo is purchasing a great many things for his new home in Greece. Furnishings of all sorts—a piano, and sofas and chairs and tables. To make his bride feel at home," he added, with a gallant little bow to Jane.

None of these items had been seen being loaded, nor had Romeo mentioned buying them. It was of his garden carriage and horses that he had spoken.

"Of course." Jane nodded.

The harder the captain explained, and he did a deal of unnecessary explaining about the cargo, the higher Renfrew's curiosity mounted. Jane, too, realized they were being led up the garden path, and determined to escape the captain to look around on her own. She wanted to indicate that Renfrew should occupy Holmes and said, with a meaningful glance, "I have seen all this before, Renfrew. I shall go up on deck and wait for you there. Perhaps it will help me get my sea legs for the voyage. You must not hurry on my account. Take your time."

Renfrew nodded his approval behind the captain's head. Holmes did not suspect a mere lady of any chicanery, and bowed her off. As soon as the saloon door was closed behind her, she scampered down the corridor, searching for stairs or a ladder below, leading to the hold. She passed many open doors, with small rooms finished in a genteel manner with varnished wainscotings and carpets, but no furniture. She assumed these were the living quarters of the occasional passenger and more privileged members of the crew.

At the farthest end of the corridor she spotted a nautical item that was half ladder, half stairway. It was like a ladder inclined as a staircase, and with a handrailing. She scurried down it and found herself in a dark passageway lit by a series of rushlights stuck into holders. At the end of the passage was another of those ladder-staircases. She descended it, too, and found a dark, narrow space, presumably leading to the hold, for she knew she had descended deep into the bowels of the ship. As she stood, trying to screw up her courage to continue, a pair of stalwart men came struggling up the ladder. They carried a heavy oaken desk, which lent credence to the captain's story of removing old lumber.

It was easy to conceal herself in the shadows, for the passage was as dark as night between the sluggish rushlights. She hoped to overhear something that would explain what was going on, but heard only the grunts of men at beasts' labor. Before she left her hiding place, she heard the scamper of feet coming down the stairs. It was two more workmen, but their load was obviously less demanding, for they had breath to speak.

"We got the soft touch this time, Scruggs." One laughed. "Old Gimpy will have a bent back after this day's work, hauling lumber, while you and me only tote bales of cotton wool."

"Aye, one thousand bales of cotton wool. I'll be ready for a pint. Make that a gallon. Fancy Lord Romeo being so daft, hiring one team to take off, and another to load on. As if one crew couldn't do both."

"Now, you wouldn't want to go putting ideas into his head. Not that there'd be room for 'em. He's all filled up with Grecian 'tiquities. What do you think the young gaffer wants with so much cotton wool?"

"Maybe Romeo's going to make Juliet spin it into gold, like Rumpelstiltskin."

"Who?"

"Ye're iggorant as a pig, Bernie. Rumpelstiltskin is a princess in a fairy tale."

They disappeared into the hold, and Jane scampered quickly along the passage, to escape before they returned. She was halfway up the ladder when she heard the heavy tread of men above. She stopped a moment, listening. There wasn't time to reach the top; she must descend again.

Behind her she heard other sounds. It was Scruggs and his ignorant friend, who had done no more than toss their bales of cotton into the hold. The steps came to a halt at the bottom of the ladder. Jane looked down over her shoulder at a pair of thugs who looked deathly dangerous. Their hair was all awry; they were dirty and beaded with perspiration from their labor, and their faces had the dumb, animal look of ruffians.

"Now, what have we got here, eh?" one of them asked.

His gloating voice filled her with dread. And already the two men above had reached the ladder. She peered up at two pairs of rough boots and fustian trousers. Her peculiar, foreshortened view gave the impression their leering faces grew out of their legs. She was trapped deep in the belly of the ship, halfway between two sets of grimy, ill-bred, and very strong-looking men. A shout would never be heard above.

"Looks like a woman to me, Scruggs," his friend answered, and laughed an oily laugh.

"No, a *lady*, Bernie. Step aside up there, lads, and let her pass, or Holmes'll have you in irons."

Jane's panic subsided to fear, and she continued her way up the ladder as fast as her hands and legs could carry her. The two men at the top stood aside politely to allow her to pass, which she did at a fast pace. "Thank you," she called over her shoulder as she tore down the corridor.

The rushlights were her sole illumination, and they showed only pale puddles of light extending no more than a few feet. But at the end of the passage was a brighter patch from the next stairway. Strange rustling sounds in the dark corners suggested the presence of rats. She gathered up her skirts and flew along. The bright patch drew closer. She was nearly at it when the rat appeared.

Jane had often seen mice. The granary at Halsey Hall was full of them. They held no terrors for her. She had always imagined a rat was only a large mouse. The creature that blocked her path, however, was no more like a mouse than a chickadee was like an eagle. It was as big as a kitten, but it was not its size that struck terror into her. It was the glittering, malevolent eye, the pointed nose and hint of sharp teeth below it, the awful stringy tail curled over its dark, humped back as it crouched, looking the very embodiment of evil. A shudder began in her stomach and reverberated through her whole body. She was not even aware that she opened her lips and emitted a piercing wail for help.

Almost immediately a pounding of feet came from behind her. Scruggs and Bernie were rushing to her aid, but by the time they arrived, the rat had escaped. Jane was trembling and pale, and looked in such danger of going into a swoon that Scruggs put a hand on her arm to steady her. On top of her fear, she now felt embarrassed at her outburst. Her wish was to escape, get out of the passage, off the ship, into Renfrew's carriage, and safely home.

Renfrew, just exiting from the saloon with Holmes, where his ingenuity had been taxed to the utmost to keep the captain engaged while Jane scouted, heard her wail and came pelting down the corridor. Holmes was not a foot behind him. They peered into the shadowy depths and saw a pale and frightened young lady, trying to detach herself from what looked very much like a dangerous attacker.

Renfrew felt an explosion in his head. Temporarily robbed of sanity, he went bucketing down the ladder and landed Scruggs a facer before anyone could explain. To add to the confusion, Holmes flew into a rage and began threatening to clamp the hapless Scruggs in irons and have him flogged.

When Renfrew grabbed Jane protectively into his arms and tried to comfort her, she found herself bursting into tears, which only made matters worse.

"My humblest apologies, Miss Halsey," Captain Holmes said. "I'll see this brute never sets foot on a ship again. Newgate is the place for him."

"Are you all right, Jane? Did he harm you?" Renfrew's concerned face leaned close to hers, and in his wildly staring eyes she read fear and pity, and an anxiety that spoke of love. His expression was strained; the painful grip he held her in showed his emotion.

Scruggs and Bernie cast an accusing eye on her, and Jane tried to explain between her tears and sobs. "No, please, don't. You don't understand. . . ."

"By God, I'll kill him." Renfrew put her aside and made a lunge at Scruggs, just picking himself up off the floor.

"No!" She grabbed his arm and stopped him. "He was trying to help me. It wasn't Scruggs."

"Eh, how'd she know me name?"

"Who attacked you, then?" Renfrew demanded. The fire in his eyes suggested he would immediately dash off and wreak revenge.

As the embarrassment of her position came over her, Jane was seized with a trembling fit that was neither tears nor laughter, but some strange admixture of the two. She was temporarily incapable of explaining.

"She's having hysterics," Holmes worried. "Best get her to my cabin. I'll send for a doctor. Who attacked her, Scruggs? Was it Gimpy?"

"I didn't see nothing. She was all alone, yelling her bloody 'ead off. Whoever done it got clean away. Couldn't of been Gimpy. He's below."

"I'll muster the men on deck and get to the bottom of this," Holmes declared, with a gruff, taking-charge manner.

Jane took a deep breath and confessed, before the whole ship was set at odds. "That won't be necessary, Captain. There was no attack. I—I saw a . . . rat." She finished on a whisper.

"A *rat!*" Three outraged voices were hurled at her. Renfrew just looked, disbelieving.

"A *huge* rat. It was looking right at me," she said, and began tidying her gown, to avoid having to look at the men.

"Did it bite you?" Holmes demanded.

"No. Scruggs rescued me before it could attack. I want to thank you, Scruggs. You were very brave."

Scruggs and Bernie exchanged a speaking glance. Holmes shook his head in mute resignation at her folly and waved the men off. Echoes of their snickers and jokes trailed behind them. "A man-eating rat," Bernie said, shaking his head. "Ye're a bloody 'ero, Scruggs. That's what you are. Heh heh heh."

Jane's cheeks were stained red with shame, but she composed her expression and said, "Shall we leave now, Renfrew? I could do with some fresh air."

"Perhaps a glass of wine . . ." he suggested.

"No! Let us go." She peered nervously around the floor for signs of a glittering eye and long tail.

"Very well. Thank you for your help, Captain," Renfrew said.

They went together to the top deck. Before they left, Holmes turned a steely eye on Miss Halsey and said, "How did it come you were below, ma'am? I understood you wanted fresh air when you left us."

She met his gaze with a firm eye. "I got lost," she replied coolly, and added "Good day, sir" before he could object to this indefensible position.

Her retreat was executed at the speed of a rout. As soon as they were on terra firma, Renfrew turned a sparkling eye on her. *"Lost?"* he asked, and fell into a spasm of laughter. "I have heard of ladies who didn't know left from right, but one who couldn't tell up from down is new to me."

"I had to say something. I don't suppose you wanted me to say I was spying to see what your imbecile brother is up to on that blasted ship."

"No, indeed. I daresay we can rule out that he is raising a colony of killer rats?"

"It's not funny, Renfrew. The brute looked vicious. It was as big as an alley cat. And it didn't even run away when I stared at it. It stood its ground. I expect it *would* have attacked if I hadn't shouted."

"And if the brave Scruggs hadn't come to your rescue. How *did* you know his name, by the by? Have you been rescued from rats before?"

She glared. "In a manner of speaking."

James read that oblique reference to his own verminous behavior, and blushed. "You do require wine. You have become irrational," he decided, and took her arm to lead her to his carriage. She shook it off, and stalked forward unaided.

Undismayed, Renfrew just watched her go. He had given up trying not to love Jane Halsey. When he had thought her in danger, he knew he was gone beyond recall. His reaction at seeing that brute's hands on her was not far from insanity. Every atom of his body had been red-hot to defend, and destroy the usurper. Which was not to say he would forgo his share of amusement at her expense, now that she was safe.

In the carriage, he took a bottle of wine and two glasses from the side pocket and proceeded to remove the cork while she looked on, determined not to be impressed at this luxurious touch of Bacchus. He poured; she accepted the glass and gulped with an unladylike haste, to steady her nerves. He poured himself a glass, and recorked the bottle.

"To your safe delivery," he said, and touched her

glass with his. "Ah, you're empty already." He poured her another glass, which she sipped more slowly.

"Shall we be getting home?" she suggested, as he had not directed the carriage forward.

"Drinking in a moving carriage is inconvenient. I told John Groom to give us ten minutes. The scenery is lovely," he mentioned, glancing out the window.

"I hope I never see another ship!"

"Then may I suggest you look out the other window, as your poor eyes are exposed to a dozen of them from that side."

Jane sipped silently a moment, then said, "All the cabins were empty."

"I beg your pardon?"

"All the cabins were empty. There was no sign of their being occupied by all those seamen he said he hired."

"They wouldn't have taken their gear on board yet."

"They didn't even have beds in them. The ship was practically stripped. He isn't hiring entertainers, or anything of that sort, as you mentioned. And the men were taking bales of cotton into the hold. They *were* removing lumber, incidentally, which looks as though Holmes said one truthful thing."

"As they were removing furniture from the hold, perhaps John Company is rearranging other furnishings as well. They're getting rid of old stuff, and shuffling the rest about to other ships. A sort of nautical housecleaning. I know Mama never buys a chair that half the house doesn't have to be rearranged. That would account for emptying the rooms. Romeo won't plan to use many cabins. But you implied the captain was lying about other things. Certainly he was trying to conceal something. We were about as welcome as a pair of lepers, but he could hardly turn the bride from the door. That, in case you wonder, is why I introduced you as Romeo's fiancée."

Jane listened, thinking her own thoughts. "Why cotton wool, Renfrew? As you said, a ship needs ballast, and Romeo didn't mention buying a piano or tables or anything of the sort. He wouldn't buy furnishings without consulting his bride, would he?"

"He considers himself quite an expert. I doubt if you'd be consulted."

"Cotton wool isn't heavy enough for ballast—is it?"

"Not unless he means to fill the hold to the rafters."

"A thousand bales. That wouldn't begin to fill it."

"Perhaps he's rented out part of the ship to carry cargo for someone. I wouldn't give him as much money as he wanted. That would be a means of making up the shortfall."

"Yes, but it sounds very practical for Romeo. I doubt he'd ever think of such a thing."

"There's a wily streak in him," Renfrew said pensively. He thought about Lady Barbara's kidnapping, and felt he ought to repeat his warning, lest Romeo had plans of carrying her off. "In fact— I don't want to alarm you, but he might not take your refusal as seriously as you hope. Something of the sort has happened before. He tried to *force* Lady Barbara into a marriage."

She turned a pair of large gray eyes on him. "What on earth are you talking about? He can't marry me without my consent."

"No, but he can make a good try." He expanded

on Lady Barbara Manfred's ordeal, which involved abduction from a ball.

She turned quite pale. "Good God. You mean he plans to kidnap me!"

"I don't say he means to, but it is a possibility you must be aware of, so you can take precautions for your own safety."

"I'll buy a pistol."

Renfrew gave her a cunning smile. "But would you really shoot him?"

"I would if he laid a hand on me."

"I doubt if he'd go that far. He *is* a gentleman, you know, and he's not violent. No, he'd dream up something craftier. Like spiriting you off to sea, and after a night alone with him—oh, quite unmolested by anything but classical quotations!—what option would you have, for the world would never believe it?"

Her lips firmed to a grim line. "I would have the option of marriage, immediately followed by widowhood! How dare he!"

"We are only discussing possibilities, Jane." The name came out nonchalantly, though not quite by accident. Renfrew wanted to speak it. And as Jane wanted to hear it, she pretended not to notice.

He refilled his glass and topped off hers. "Feeling better now?" he asked. "It was unforgivable of me to let you wander off on your own. I should have gone myself."

"If you say you're not afraid of rats, James!"

The soft smile that caressed her showed his pleasure at their having reached a first-name basis, without the formality of discussing it. "What astonishes me is that you weren't afraid of Scruggs and company. Now, there was something to fear."

"Oh, they were harmless. They're robbing Romeo

blind—it is the custom, apparently, for one crew to both remove the old cargo and put on the new—but outside of a little larceny, they're all right. They don't know why he's taking on the cotton wool either. They spoke as though the wool were Romeo's. It is very odd, is it not?"

"I'm just relieved he's not refitting the entire vessel. He spoke of your desire for a bed canopied in velvet. The tableware, too, fell under your opprobrium, he claimed. Can't say I blame you. I could scarcely lift the cup, and it was empty." A jeering smile accompanied the speech.

"Did he say so indeed? *He* is the one who wanted velvet canopies. I preferred the bunks."

"He might have taken your refusal more seriously had you expressed your aversion to the entire scheme, rather than preferring bunks. That suggests acceptance in principle, surely."

"You're as bad as your brother. You twist everything around. Why do you not take me home? My head is splitting."

"You shouldn't drink so much," Renfrew said with mock sternness. He opened the window and emptied her glass on the ground, pulled the checkstring, and they were off.

As the carriage lumbered through the streets, he cleared his throat and said, "About that night, Jane . . ."

Jane rearranged her gloves and said stiffly, "The less said about it, the better. I was out-of-reason cross when I heard you scheming to palm Romeo off on me. I daresay I said more than I ought to have."

"I shouldn't have encouraged him in the first place."

Her silent reply was mirrored in her eyes. Or me! You shouldn't have encouraged *me*.

"It's just that he—we hoped he would settle down," he said.

"Just so you realize he will not be settling down with me," she answered sharply.

It was obviously not the moment to put forth his own case. "Yes, I'm sorry. It was foolish of me."

"Foolish?" She turned a wrathful countenance on him. "It was *infamous*!"

Before the conversation degenerated into tears, Renfrew spoke of other things, and Miss Halsey reached home with dry eyes.

Chapter Eleven

CONCERN FOR Jane's safety at the hands of Lord Romeo made an unexceptional excuse for Renfrew to haunt the little house on Catherine Street. He returned the next afternoon, and found Belle and Jane hemming handkerchiefs for Basil. As Mrs. Pettigrew was playing propriety, he said nothing about his brother.

"You ladies are wasting a beautiful day," he said, glancing through the curtains to the sun-dappled street.

Mrs. Pettigrew felt quite at home with fine lords by this time, and said with no ceremony that as sure as they had the team put to, they would end up on Bond Street, and once ladies were let loose on Bond Street, they would only end up spending money they didn't have. "Once Basil's position is raised, of course, we will be higher in the stirrups," she added hopefully.

Renfrew failed to recognize the hint. "There is the park. A drive through it is free," he pointed out. It was his goal to drive Jane out; his problem was that he preferred to do it without the chaperon.

"I must have been through Hyde Park a hundred times," Mrs. Pettigrew said, and tied a knot in her thread. "But if you girls would like to borrow the carriage, I'm sure you have only to say so. A pity Basil cannot join you."

"I am just on my way there. Why do you not accompany me, and save Mrs. Pettigrew's team?" Renfrew said, trying for an impromptu air.

Belle's wish was to give her sister free rein with Renfrew, and she said, "You go along, Jane. I'll help Aunt Pettigrew finish the hemming."

"Then I shall stay home, too. Thank you, Renfrew," Jane said. She had no intention of running after him. She had mistaken his friendship for love before, and was not about to repeat her error.

Renfrew accepted defeat like a gentlemen, which is to say gracefully, but with no intention of giving up. "Perhaps another time, when you are less busy." He nodded.

The ladies returned the nod, and offered their caller a glass of wine. Just before leaving he said nonchalantly, "Ah, about our drive . . . shall we say . . . tomorrow, around three?"

"I shall be playing cards, but you girls might as well go," Mrs. Pettigrew suggested.

Jane nodded with no particular display of the excitement she was feeling. Immediately after the caller had left, Belle arose and laid down her sewing. "I must speak to Munch about our silk stockings for the duchess's rout." Before leaving the room, she gave Jane an imperative look, and ere long, Jane, too, found an excuse to go upstairs.

Miss Munch had already been informed of the call and the projected outing. "I shan't go with you tomorrow" were Belle's first words when her sister entered. "Renfrew wants to drive out with you, Jane. It was perfectly clear what he was up to, only he was too polite to say it."

Although Jane entertained a similar hope, she said calmly, "You are putting too much meaning into the invitation, Belle. Renfrew is neither shy nor reticent. If he wished to drive out with me, he would have said so. We both go, or neither of us goes." When Jane spoke in that firm voice, there was no hope of moving her.

Belle knew it, but she made one more effort. "But he never took his eyes off you, Jane. That is, he glanced at Aunt Pettigrew and me from time to time, but it was plain as a pikestaff it was you he wanted to see. His head kept turning back to you as if it were on a pivot. You should have seen him, Munch."

Jane just silently shook her head.

"If he has an offer to make, let him make it" was Miss Munch's opinion. "I'd have no truck with a gentleman who blows hot and cold. Who is to say he ain't in league with his loony brother? He might plan to deliver Jane right into the hole of that boat, to be wafted off to grease. The whole family is in collision for all we know. Why else is a duchess inviting you all to tea, and to fancy balls? And how about your petticoat, Miss Halsey? Do I put on the new row of lace, or will you save the lace for your second-best blue gown?"

"The blue gown. It won't show on a petticoat."

"Unless we made a ruches up at the hem here and there, like page seven of *La Belle Assemblée*."

The periodical was so thumbed it fell open at the favorite page, and Jane's attention was temporarily diverted to this important decision. But as she gazed with unseeing eyes at the picture, she felt more interest in Renfrew's intentions than she pretended. His regard had seemed rather warm the day before at the ship. Nor was she unaware that he had often gazed in her direction that afternoon. Warmth and gazing were all well and good, but unless he said in unequivocal terms that he cared for her, she would not reveal her feelings again.

She felt hot with shame when she recalled how often in the past she had betrayed herself. On how many occasions had she assumed he would stand up first with her, and even mentioned it? She had also assumed Renfrew had asked Romeo to take her to Whitehall to hear him speak, and on that occasion, too, she had been mistaken. He had invited her and Belle out tomorrow, and if Belle declined, she would do likewise.

The matter was decided that evening before they retired. With an air of unconcern Jane said, as she drew back the top sheet, "We haven't decided about tomorrow, Belle. Are you quite determined to decline? I should rather like a drive in the park, if you would accompany us."

"Yes, of course I shall," Belle replied artlessly, and blew out the candle.

She knew Jane's determination, and had formed her plan. Basil was directed to leave some papers at home. Belle was to "discover" them, and call to Mrs. Pettigrew's mind that he required those papers that very afternoon. Their aunt was sufficiently keen on Basil's career that she would want the papers taken to him. What more natural than that the drive to Hyde Park should take a detour to Burlington House? Belle would say in her most innocent voice that there was that painting of Halsey Hall Basil particularly wanted to show her, and would it be too terribly inconvenient for Renfrew to return and pick her up in forty-five minutes? Jane couldn't read her a lecture in front of him, and with luck, she would not be in a mood to do so after the drive. Belle was hoping Jane would have other things on her mind, like announcing an offer of marriage.

All began well according to plan. Belle was careful not to "discover" the papers till Renfrew's carriage had stopped outside the door. Mrs. Pettigrew flew into spasms of alarm. Renfrew was extremely gracious about going out of his way to stop at Burlington House. The plan came close to going awry when he also offered to take the papers in to Basil. "No need for you to disturb yourself, Miss Belle. Let me do it," he said, reaching for the papers.

Belle launched into her rehearsed speech, which Jane heard with dilating nostrils. "The picture of Halsey Hall, you mean, Belle? I would like to see it, too."

"No, no. It is really nothing out of the ordinary. It is probably not of Halsey Hall at all. Basil only mentioned a resemblance. It is not worth your while," Belle countered.

Renfrew looked hopeful, and even tried to catch Jane's eye. She refused to regard him. "I would very much like to see it, if Renfrew doesn't mind waiting a moment?" Jane said, and repeated again when Belle assured her it wasn't worth a glance. "It won't take us a moment."

"Let us all have a look at it, then," Renfrew said impatiently. "We've wasted more than a moment talking about it." The edge in his voice was caused by Jane's refusing to take advantage of the proffered privacy.

"If you are in a hurry to get to Hyde Park, pray don't feel obliged to wait for us," Jane sniped.

"How did you plan to get back home if I left you here?"

"I believe Basil would see us home."

Belle saw her scheme was having wretched results and exclaimed, "Oh, never mind. The papers aren't that important or Basil would have sent home for them."

Renfrew said through thin lips, "We shall deliver the papers, and see the painting that looks something like your home."

"Well, let us deliver the papers first," Belle said, in a very small, apologetic voice.

By this time Jane was determined not to spend one fraction of a second alone with Renfrew and said, "We'll all go."

She accompanied Belle down the familiar corridor, with Renfrew a step behind them. Jane tapped at the door and stared in chagrin when Lord Romeo opened it. He looked over her shoulder to Jane, and a smile beamed on his face.

"Athene! The gods are kind to me today."

It was all that was needed to put the cap on an appalling outing. "Romeo!" Her greeting had much the air of a complaint.

Basil said in a perfectly audible aside to Belle, "I thought you were coming alone!"

Jane felt humiliated. It appeared as though the whole family had been scheming to throw her at Renfrew's head. Belle's whispered reply was indistinguishable, but it didn't take a genius to realize what she had been up to. Basil invited them all into a cubbyhole that accommodated two fairly comfortably. The ladies were given the chairs, while the three gentlemen stood, shuffling their feet and glaring at one another. The major object of Romeo's displeasure was his brother.

"Captain Holmes tells me you went to visit *Justice*," he said. "I trust you have received my letter of protest in that regard. A gentleman waits to be invited before he goes barging into a man's home, James, and at the moment, that ship is my home. You would not likely have noticed, but I did not return home last night. I have directed my valet to remove my personal effects to the *Justice*. If the duchess chances to notice her youngest son is missing, you may tell her where I am now residing."

James felt the full humiliation of having his bizarre family circumstances flaunted in public. It was obvious from the astonished blinks of all the auditors that they found it nearly incredible. His reply was brusque. "What the devil are you doing here?"

"Why did you write Renfrew a letter? Why didn't you just speak to him, since he is your brother?" Belle asked.

"I do not speak to my family," Romeo told her. "Actually you did hear me speak to Lord Renfrew just now, but I lost my head. Perhaps you would tell him for me that I am not speaking to him."

Belle just stared from one to the other. Jane was more familiar with the young man's strange ways. She had seen enough of him to recognize a certain slyness in his smile. What is he up to? she wondered. She thought if Renfrew were allowed to speak to his brother without the embarrassment of being ignored, he would persist in asking Romeo what he was doing here. Was that why Romeo had decided they weren't speaking, because he was concealing something? She decided to repeat the question herself. "What are you doing here, Romeo?" she inquired.

"I spend a deal of time here, giving Herb a hand assembling the rubble of the Parthenon."

"I thought it was all packed up to be moved to the British Museum."

"You don't imagine I could entrust such a perilous expedition to amateurs! I am overseeing the entire operation. Your cousin will tell you I have added many excellent suggestions to the packing."

Basil said a few enthusiastic words of agreement.

"I personally wrapped Thalia's head in goose feathers," Romeo continued. He had a way of taking the conversation in hand and directing it toward his own peculiar interests. "Oh, I know it was an extravagance, but Thalia is something very special to me. Shredded paper is sufficient for the larger pieces, so long as they are double-wrapped in canvas and placed in tightly fitting boxes. Really rather amusing, they look like coffins, all lined up and waiting for the charnel house. It is a queer mixture of coffins for giants and midgets, for long, lean chaps and square, tubby persons. As you are interested in my work, Athene, come along and I shall show you my precautions."

He led her into the corridor, and as she wished a few moments privacy with him, she went without argument. With a possessive hand on her elbow, he took her to where the Marbles stood, packed and ready for shipment.

"Now, this long, lean fellow I call Lord Castlereagh," he said. "Envisaging a suitably sized corpse in each box helps me to remember what is in the container. I must confess it also pleases me to imagine having such irritants in their coffins. Castlereagh is a bit of architrave. And beneath him goes the Cabinet," he said, pointing to a larger box. "It, of course, is the matching entablature, bearing a miscellany of lesser gods. I have each of the ministers boxed up individually as well, along with the royal family. That particularly monumental carton you are examining is Prinny. The choice was between him and the prime minister, Liverpool. I opted for royalty. Outside of the entablature, there isn't another container so large in the collection. It is a highly embellished piece of frieze. Not in such good repair as it ought to be. I trust the analogy is obvious to you?"

"Yes, I see what you are about."

"It will help to put the exhibition back together again at the museum as well. I have given names that associate the proper bits and pieces in the proper order. The royal statues are named chronologically—George, Frederick, William, Charlotte, etc."

"You plan to stay in London long enough to help with the sorting, do you?"

"I hope to, but Herb knows my system, in any case."

A pair of workmen came by and tugged their forelocks to Romeo. "Where should we put the dook, sir?" one of them asked.

"Ah, Wellington. Zeus," he explained aside to Jane. "Place him in front of Prinny. That should give the rest of the boxes an argument worth listening to. And mind you, lay it down carefully, lads."

This all seemed harmless enough, and fairly typical of Romeo. Jane was more interested in other matters. She wished to introduce her queries in an innocent fashion, however, and said, "Did you know there are rats on the *Justice*, Romeo?"

"That, too, seems highly symbolic, does it not? But I have this very morning had the rat catcher in to rid the ship of them, as Holmes told me they disconcert you. You need not fear they will molest you."

"Naturally that doesn't concern me, as it is doubtful I shall ever be on the ship again. I want to make very clear, Romeo, that I am not marrying you."

"Ladies have changed their minds before."

"I shan't, and I don't intend to be taken aboard by force either."

"They have told you about my tendresse for the Barbarian." Jane looked curious. "It is my pet name for Lady Barbara. Lord Renfrew, I expect, is your informant?" He pinned her with a piercing gaze.

"He mentioned it."

"I wonder why." His satiric smile suggested jealousy was at the bottom of it. "History has many repetitions of inferior brothers resenting their superiors. Excellence in an outsider they can tolerate, but when it occurs en famille, it must seem a reproach. Renfrew vexes me, and you vex me, Athene, to accuse me of repetition. When a ruse proves ineffective, I have the wits to abandon it. Kidnapping a bride requires a coldness and cruelty that are alien to my pacific nature. I use the siren's wiles these days, not the warrior's might."

"Did you hope to lure me with bales of cotton?" she teased, and listened closely for his reply.

"Ah, no, they have a more practical use. Cotton is in high demand in Greece. I bought them for a pittance, and shall sell them to merchants in Athens for a large profit. Other items in high demand will be joining the cotton in the hold. You will find silk and brandy, along with some more bourgeois items, such as potatoes and a variety of grains. Everything but owls. That is a joke, Athene. To carry owls to Athens is like carrying coals to Newcastle."

"Oh, really?"

He stared at her ignorance. "Never mind, I shall educate you. After we are settled into marriage, I daresay we shall find the nights long and dull enough, but at least we shan't sit staring with glazed eyes at a journal, and talking about the servants, like my parents. You have much to learn."

"How the devil should I know there are owls in Greece? I don't know anything about it."

"And you seem remarkably determined not to learn. Greece is a rocky, barren place. There is not much there, outside of the owls and goats. But the water and rocks are lovely."

"It sounds bleak."

"Never; the sun always shines. There are incredible outcroppings of wildflowers, defying nature and growing out of rocky hills. But why do we waste precious moments speaking of rocks and water? Let us speak of nectar and hyacinths, of moonlight and dancing."

"Ah, dancing!" she exclaimed, and seized the chance to divert the conversation. "Will you be attending your mother's party?"

"Certainly, I would never offend Terpsichore by a refusal. I have already told you the party is in my honor. I have sent in my acceptance."

Another workman approached them. "Do you want Lady Jersey with Wellington and his lot, or does she go with the other ladies?"

"My dear chap, don't be ridiculous. What use would Lady Jersey have for ladies? Put her with the gentlemen, where she will feel at home."

The workman eyed the corridor, which was littered with cartons. "We're getting crowded here. There's an empty room down at the end of the hallway."

"No, we want all the cartons as near the doorway as possible, for easy loading on the wagons. The likeliest time for an accident is when they are being handled by men."

The workman gave a dismissing shrug. "We handle them now or we handle them later. No matter to me."

"But later there will be confusion. Let us establish order while it is still possible," Romeo said patiently.

The man nodded and left.

"Have you set even a tentative date for your departure, Romeo?" Jane asked.

He hesitated a moment, which gave her pause. "When I have placed the Marbles in their new home, I shall catch the first prevailing breeze to Greece. Must I really sail alone, Athene?" He reached out and took her two hands in his.

Romeo wore a wistful, slightly accusing expression. Jane no longer thought he had any nefarious designs on her. He had explained any seeming mystery regarding his ship, and as her concern dissipated, she began to feel sorry for him.

"Why don't you remain in England, Romeo?"

"I must go to Greece, but that is not to say I shall stay there forever. Perhaps you will miss me. I shall write, and if you find you care for me, I shall return for you, my Athene."

On this tender speech, he raised her hand to his lips, to kiss each finger separately. She was first touched, but as he lingered over his occupation, and switched methodically from right hand to left and started the procedure again, she became impatient with him. That was the trouble with Romeo: He had to overdo everything. In the end she pulled her hand away briskly.

"Let us return to Basil's office. It is time we were leaving."

"It is kind of you to indicate a desire for my presence, Athene, but I cannot accompany you. I have work that must be done here. With fortune, even this short absence will work in my favor. I must confess, however, I have not yet arranged your velvet-canopied bed."

"Don't buy any velvet on my account, Romeo."

"You are right, as usual. What need have we for velvet? We shall make love in the open, beneath the laughing moon and sighing stars. Did Zeus wait for a canopied bed to rape Leda? Did Pluto for Persephone? Or Paris for Helen? But I ought not to have mentioned kidnapping. How the Greeks do love a challenge, though. Nothing makes a lady so irresistible as her belonging to someone else. I daresay that was Helen's major attraction."

"It is not an attraction that bedizens me. I belong to no man."

"Very true. That independence is *your* attraction, Athene. A virgin queen, like Bess. That, too, presents a challenge, you must know."

He bowed and left. Jane returned to Basil's office, where the others awaited her. Renfrew stood gazing out the window, and the others sat, looking bored. "Shall we go and see the picture now?" she asked.

"We've already seen it," Belle said. "It doesn't look much like Halsey Hall after all. Let us go on to Hyde Park."

When they were finally in the carriage and driving toward the park, Renfrew said, "Had Romeo anything interesting to say?"

"Perhaps, if I could only figure out what he is ever talking about." Jane repeated his notion of keeping track of the cartons by giving them names.

"That won't be much help to Pettigrew," Renfrew mentioned.

"Oh, Romeo plans to remain for the unpacking."

"When is the move to be made, exactly?"

Jane and Belle had heard a good deal about this from Basil, and could tell him unequivocally that it was to begin the following Monday morning at nine o'clock.

"So Romeo cannot be planning to leave till later in the week." He looked uncertainly at Jane. This seemed a long time for her to have to worry about her safety.

"You could write him a letter and inquire," Belle suggested.

"If it is me you're worried about," Jane said, "I don't believe he plans anything like a forcible abduction."

"And even if he did, he wouldn't do it till moments before he lifted anchor," Renfrew added.

"He assured me he would not," she said, frowning in uncertainty. "Really, he seems entirely preoccupied with the move of the Marbles."

"That's rather strange, too. I had to twist his arm to get him to even go and look at them."

'One look and he was smitten," Jane said, shaking her head in amusement.

The outing that had given so little pleasure to this point became less prickly. The group descended from the carriage at the park and walked a little. Belle made frequent short excursions to examine a bush or squirrel on her own, to allow the others privacy, whether they wanted it or not.

In a more benign mood, Jane didn't insist on trailing at her sister's heels. "It seems I must guard you for another week," Renfrew said, smiling to show there was some romance in the speech.

The toss of Jane's head was a very model of flirtation. "Not at all. Romeo forgets all about me, till I happen to meet him somewhere by chance. He never comes to call."

"That exclamation of delight when he saw you at Basil's office, though—that didn't sound like uninterest."

"Perhaps you could tell me the trick of alienating him, as you have had such singular success in that direction. Does he *really* write letters to you, Renfrew?"

"Certainly, he does. He likes any excuse to set pen to paper. Romeo is quite a Renaissance man. He paints, writes, sculpts, as well as involving himself in architecture."

"He also has a head for business," she said, and explained about the cargo he was taking to Greece for profit.

"Let us agree he is a paragon, and have done with it. I have had enough of Lord Romeo for one day."

The remainder of the outing was pleasant, without reaching any outstanding heights of euphoria. Belle taxed her ingenuity to the limit, but eventually ran out of bushes and squirrels, and had to rejoin the party.

When the ladies were returned to Catherine Street, they had some privacy till Mrs. Pettigrew returned from her card game.

"Did Renfrew say anything?" Belle asked as soon

as the door was closed behind them. Her eyes shone with eager interest.

"He said a great many things. And now I have something to say to you, miss. I was mortified at that spectacle at Burlington House, Belle. How did you come to do such a thing?"

"But did he ask you to marry him?"

"Of course not!"

Belle's face clouded over. "Oh, I thought he might. If you had gone on with him when we stopped at Burlington House—"

"Renfrew is not a helpless child. If he wants to marry me, he will make his own opportunity to ask."

"Is he returning tomorrow?" Belle asked hopefully.

"No, he mentioned the Corn Bill is being debated in the House. He must be there."

"At least he has an unexceptionable excuse."

"He doesn't need an excuse! Really, Belle. I wish you would stop this."

"Or maybe he'll write a letter, like Romeo," Belle said, and went laughing upstairs to discuss the affair with Miss Munch.

"The boy sounds like a knock-in-the-cradle" was Munch's opinion of a man who wrote letters to his own family, residing under the same roof. When she was informed he had moved out of the house onto a ship, she threw up her hands in despair.

"He behaves more like a yahoo than a decent human bean. Come on and have a look at the blue gown. I pinned up a couple of ruches. If you like the effect, I'll sew them."

Chapter Twelve

*T*HE AFTERNOON of the duchess's rout, three corsages were received at Catherine Street for the ladies. They were not, however, addressed one to each lady. Jane received two, Belle one, and Mrs. Pettigrew none. Romeo sent Jane a hyacinth, surrounded by smaller blooms, but still any flower of the bulb family made a peculiar corsage, no matter how artfully it was disguised. Though it smelled lovely, she refused to pin anything so outré to her gown. Renfrew sent the more traditional ornament of baby roses, one corsage in pink, the other in red. As the enclosed card was addressed to the Misses Halsey, Jane didn't know which was hers.

She was faced with the dilemma of choosing. To wear Renfrew's roses would not only show a partiality for him, it would offend Romeo, and an offended Romeo might be capable of any folly. On the other hand, she had no more desire to encourage Romeo than to be seen at a public rout wearing a tuber.

"How vexing!" she said. "If I wear Renfrew's, it will look as though I prefer him."

"But surely you do," Belle pointed out. She had already chosen the pink corsage for herself, and was trying it against her white gown.

"Wear them both," Munch advised Jane, "both the pretty-smelling little lilies and the red roses."

"I'd look like a waltzing flower garden." A red corsage ill-suited Jane's yellow silk. "I shall give Aunt Pettigrew the red roses and wear no corsage," she decided.

"If you want to go to the party looking like you haven't a suitor to your name, it's no concern of mine," Munch averred, though her flashing eye belied the sentiment. She stuck the hyacinth in a vase, where its cloying perfume was a constant reminder to the recipient of what faced her that evening.

Only Mrs. Pettigrew was completely happy with the corsages, for she was unaware that she received hers at second hand. "Lord Renfrew is a real gentleman, sending flowers to your chaperon, girls." She smiled complacently. "I haven't received flowers since my husband died, and it was a rare enough occurrence then." Basil looked conscious of having failed in his filial duties, and squirmed uncomfortably.

The evening that stretched before Jane offered some hope of pleasure, even without a corsage. A rout party at the home of a duchess was unusual enough to excite her, but there were a few pitfalls yawning, too. Most of them centered around Romeo. How would he behave? Would he make her an object of fun in front of the *ton* of London? She could hardly hope he would ignore her. At the bottom of her heart she longed for some distinguishing gallantry from Renfrew, but that might very well precipitate a wrestling match in her honor. A nagging ache pinched at her temples before ever she left the house.

It did not diminish when she saw the duchess's idea of "a small dinner party" included two tables of twenty-four each. Renfrew was to be host of one table, his mother of the other. Jane looked with interest to see which table she was assigned to, and also to see where Romeo was to be seated. The first surprise was that he had not come to dinner. The second, and it was not only a surprise but a deep disappointment, was that she was not at Renfrew's table.

The duchess got her aside on the way into the dining room and said, "I fear my son has shabbed off. When Romeo wrote, he did not actually say he would come to dinner. He will not touch meat, you must know, which makes serving him awkward. Very likely that is why he stayed away, but he has assured me he would be here for the dance. He was to sit at the foot of my table, Miss Halsey, which is why you are placed there, beside an empty chair. I trust you will not take offense at being below the salt, now that you know the reason."

Jane heard all this with a falling heart. The duchess obviously thought she was Romeo's intended. Equally obvious was that Renfrew had not indicated otherwise. He had no interest in her himself, then. She had been reading too much into his manner. Her eyes strayed to the other table, where they encountered a beautiful young blond Incomparable sitting at Renfrew's right hand. Belle and Mrs. Pettigrew were halfway down the board. The only thing that made the dinner possible was that Basil was Jane's partner, so she did not have to worry about making polite conversation.

Basil was a veritable chatterbox throughout dinner. While Jane toyed with her soup, and picked a little at her turbot, he was busy to point out the various gentlemen present who might help him in his career. "Do you realize, Jane, there are four Cabinet ministers at this party, and Renfrew isn't even a Tory? I feared the evening would be a dead loss, but it is nothing of the sort. I shall scrape an acquaintance with Bathurst before the evening is over. If I could twist the chancellor's arm to get more funds for the museum, it wouldn't do me any harm either."

"That's wonderful, Basil. I wonder where Romeo is. Was he at Burlington House this afternoon?"

"Yes, he was still there when I left. He is a wonderful help. I don't know how I should have gone on without him."

"I think his system of naming the cartons is rather whimsical. Would it not have been easier to number them?"

"But they *are* numbered. What do you mean, naming them?"

Jane explained what Romeo had told her. Basil shook his head. "That may be his system. He is so erudite he could do something like that. I assure you all those Grecian names mean very little to me. I have put numbers on every carton. I do not rely totally on Romeo, for there is no saying he will still be here when the unpacking is done. He mentioned sailing with the first favorable breeze."

"Oh, no, the first favorable breeze *after* you are unpacked. He will not leave you in the lurch."

"You must have misunderstood. There was a fellow at Burlington House this very afternoon with a load of foodstuff for the *Justice*. Fruits and vegetables—fresh produce would not be put on board a week in advance."

There was an eruption of merriment from Renfrew's table, and Jane's attention was diverted from talk of Romeo. "Do you happen to know the lady at Renfrew's right hand?" she asked.

"That is Lady Sylvia Challoner, the Season's Incomparable. Incredible she didn't accept an offer. She was probably holding out for Renfrew. He looks suitably smitten, *n'est-ce pas*? Not that she can count on an offer. He is a notorious flirt. According to Romeo, he goes through half a dozen ladies in a Season."

Renfrew chanced to turn toward the other table at that moment, and received such a blazing scowl from Miss Halsey that he hardly knew what to make of it. He was having his own share of vexation. For Mama to have seated Lady Sylvia on his right hand indicated an intimacy that did not exist. He had been one of Sylvia's flirts early in the Season, but time and proximity had cooled his ardor. He wondered, too, at Romeo's absence, and was on nettles lest the boy was out arranging to have Jane kidnapped.

Lady Sylvia had already superseded any other ladies for Renfrew's first dance. He had hoped Romeo would have that one with Jane, so he might claim her for the second. This party had been a wretched idea. He should have forbidden it. His mother was completely convinced Miss Halsey would rescue Romeo from insanity, and had quite set her heart on a match in that quarter. He must bide his time, and let her see Jane had no intention of marrying his brother. After Romeo had set sail for Greece, his own romance could advance in the normal way. To push it forward now would only excite his mother's unstable temper. She would be less than kind to Jane in that event. Romeo was quite adamant about leaving England, and after the past few weeks of nonsensical behavior, James was becoming resigned to it. Indeed he looked forward with considerable impatience to the launching of the *Justice*.

The dinner hour seemed long, but eventually even two courses and two removes were over, and the ladies escaped to the saloon to allow the gentlemen privacy for their port. Mrs. Pettigrew and her nieces sat together, feeling like Methodists at an Anglican picnic, for they knew very few of the guests except their hostess, and she was caught up in another group. The interval was passed by Jane's relating to Mrs. Pettigrew what Basil had said over dinner, and each lady telling the others the names of any guests she had managed to identify. This occupation was not sufficient to prevent Jane from making a detailed inventory of Lady Sylvia's toilette, which proved to be as incomparable as everything about the lady.

In due time the gentlemen entered the saloon, and the Halseys watched with bated breath to see which group Renfrew honored with his company. They felt neither joy nor grief but only a dull disappointment when he was waylaid by his mother. Lady Sylvia soon added herself to the grouping, but the initiative was hers. Renfrew had not gone to her. Jane discerned the sly grins and whispered comments at Lady Sylvia's pushing herself forward, and felt a reproach in every look. Just so had she chased Renfrew in the past. If his friends were amused at the attentions of Lady Sylvia, a noble Incomparable and an heiress, how they must have stared at *her* presumption. She took what consolation she could from the one look Renfrew conferred on her. It was a small, impatient smile, directed over Lady Sylvia's shoulder.

After-dinner guests began arriving for the rout, and the host and hostess left the saloon to welcome them. The dinner guests began drifting in threes and fours to the ballroom. Mrs. Pettigrew fell into conversation with an elderly widow and remained behind. Basil escorted the young ladies to the dance. Jane, with a sort of emotional compass, immediately discovered Renfrew, standing up with Lady Sylvia. With this to firm her resolve, she accepted the first person who asked to partner her for the next set.

It was Sir Dabney Porter, an unprepossessing gentleman of small physical distinction but great wealth, who bowed and mumbled and finally made clear his intention. "Next set . . . beg the pleasure . . . unless it's a waltz. Can't waltz. Two left feet . . . bit of a dab at the jig, though."

Anything was better than being left sitting alone. Jane would have accepted if he had been Jack Ketch. Sir Dabney joined them to await the next set. His bulging blue eyes alighted on Belle, and what little conversation he possessed deserted him. He was struck mute at such a vision of glory. Jane had to tell him when the next sets began forming. As Belle and Basil were part of the set, Sir Dabney went along without urging. His passion for Belle invaded his feet, and his dancing became even more erratic than his halting conversation.

Jane never thought she would be happy to see Lord Romeo devouring her with his eyes, but when she spied his angelic face in the doorway, gazing at her, she welcomed the sight. Her smile was sufficient encouragement for Romeo to advance in mid-set and claim her. He was light on his feet, and managed to slide into the set during an interchange of partners during the quadrille. When Sir Dabney reached for Jane's hand, Romeo was there before him. A false step during a dance was nothing new for Sir Dabney. He reached for the next lady, and found her hand occupied, too. He continued around the square till at last he realized he was de trop, and retired to the corner, rubbing his head in confusion.

"This square was already complete, Romeo," Jane pointed out. "You should not have barged in. What will Sir Dabney think?"

"He didn't look like a deep thinker to me."

"You were late arriving," Jane said. "I hope you realize you left me without a dinner partner by your tardiness."

"You noticed!"

"It's rather hard not to notice an empty chair. You should have let your mother know you were delayed. It was thoughtless of you."

"That is twice you've used the word *should* inside of a minute. It is my second most despised word in the English language, immediately after *can't*. I didn't tell her I would attend dinner. Mama invariably serves a saddle of mutton. She knows my aversion to eating dead animals. And now it is your turn to explain yourself, Athene. Where is your hyacinth?"

"At home in a vase."

"You share my aversion, then."

"To killing flowers?"

"No, to the degradation of the hyacinth."

Miss Halsey stared in confusion. "What has it done, that you speak so harshly of it?"

"The question is rather what has been done to it. My poor gift bears small resemblance to the splendid crimson bloom that sprung from the ground from Hyacinthus' blood. Struck a fatal blow by Apollo's errant discus. A less than heroic way to die, though honorable. Where is James?"

Already Jane had forgotten her first pleasure at seeing a familiar face, and was beginning to find Romeo tedious. "Why—did you want to send him a letter?" she asked curtly.

"No, I want to shake hands, and make it up with him. I shall forgive Mama before I leave as well. Leave the party, I mean," he added hastily.

"I am happy to hear it. What has brought about this change of heart?

"Lovers—and heroes—ought to be generous."

She mistrusted the twinkle in his eye, and had no intention of pursuing this perilous subject. There was an air of nervousness about Romeo that worried her. She sensed some tension coiling in him. Upon closer examination she saw it was not a twinkle in his eye; it was a febrile glitter. Something also caused a slight flush on his usually pale face. Her major fear regarding Romeo was that he might try to kidnap her. When she remembered Basil's remark that perishable food was sent to the *Justice* that afternoon, her fears escalated.

"I see Herb is here," he said after glancing around the floor.

"Yes." She was on the verge of inquiring about the food delivery when she changed her mind. It might be best not to alert him to her suspicions. As she recalled her talk with Basil, she remembered as well that there was some uncertainty as to just when Romeo meant to sail. Basil had mentioned the first fair breeze—and there was a good breeze tonight, unhampered by clouds or any sign of storm. Was that why Romeo wanted to patch up the quarrel with his family? Every sign pointed to an immediate departure. A nervousness came over her. She felt she should tell someone her suspicions. The person who came to mind was Renfrew.

A second thought told her Basil was her nominal protector. He and his mother should be told, but still her instinct was to run straight to Renfrew. She rationalized that Romeo was his younger brother after all, and he naturally had no desire for a scandal in the family.

"I approve of Herb," Romeo continued. "He will make a charming brother-in-law."

"Charming, but he has no sister, Romeo."

An impish smile beamed. "You are being pedantic, Athene. Cousin-in-law is what I mean. You know whom I plan to marry."

Her nervousness escalated to a quaking inside. His speech was as good as a confession. "And you know whom I do not want to marry," she reminded him.

"That quavering voice is as good as an acceptance. Like Terence, I know the disposition of women. When you will, they won't; when you won't, they set their hearts upon you. But there is no time for coyness, Athene. Soon I shall be gone. Can I leave you here to pine away without me? Greeks love a challenge—I share that with them, but their notions of revenge exceed mine. I could not be so cruel. You will accompany me," he said, not forcefully, nor jokingly. He just said it, as though he were saying "It's a nice evening." As though protestations were vain. The matter was settled.

Jane was saved the embarrassment of running after Renfrew. Romeo spotted him across the floor, smiled and bowed, and at once the brothers began pacing toward each other, to meet in the middle of the floor.

"Good evening, Romeo. You're late," Renfrew said, but in a perfectly friendly spirit.

"Don't hector me, James. I am here, bearing an olive branch. Young men's minds are always changeable, and I have given over hating you. There is a fullness of all things, even of hate. I shall probably be leaving within the week, and want to stitch up the rift in our family."

"Have you set a date?" Renfrew asked.

"Ah, how I look forward to the voyage. A ship swift as a bird, skimming over wine-dark seas. When gray-eyed Athene sends a favorable breeze, a fresh west wind, I shall be off."

"A west wind won't take you far. It's a southeast wind you need." Renfrew laughed.

"Don't be so literal. Do you not recognize the immortal prose of Homer? It will not be necessary for you to remind me he is an epic poet. The translations into English reduce him to prose. I am thinking of doing a proper translation when I get home."

"So you really are leaving," Renfrew said ruefully.

"I am, but you must waste no new tears over old griefs. I can love England from abroad. At closer hand, her faults are too overpowering. England is quite like a lady in that respect, is she not?" His gaze flickered over Miss Halsey.

Jane glanced at Renfrew, and saw the laughing light in his eyes. She tossed her curls and said to Romeo, "You, sir, are no gentleman!"

"Come, come, my pet. Present company is always excepted. How you ladies angle for a compliment. Even you, Athene, who ought to soar above such common tricks."

Renfrew looked an apology for his brother's out-spokenness. "Will you speak to Mama?" he asked his brother.

"I shall obey the primeval law. Hatred never ceases by hatred, so I shall forgive her."

"You really go a bit far to charge that Mama hates you, Romeo."

"For a mother to withhold love is tantamount to hatred. Of course she was always an unnatural parent. I bore too little resemblance to a colt to please her. You were more fortunate in that respect."

James ignored the embroidery and went to the main point. "She does love you. She'd show you, if you'd let her."

"This will be her opportunity for fifteen years of neglect," he said, and strolled off in search of the duchess.

Renfrew looked helplessly after him. "He means no harm, you know," he apologized. "Romeo was sent to Greece for his health when he was a boy. Every care was taken for his physical well-being, but it is clear he missed his family, and felt abandoned. He has used the phrase 'happily abandoned,' and would not return when he was cured, so . . ."

"I daresay there is a reason why he is so—different, but I wouldn't be too sure he means no harm," Jane cautioned. "We must speak in private, James."

His expression sharpened to anxiety. "Why? What has he done?"

"Nothing—yet."

Without further ado he took her hand and they hurried to a private sitting room, where Jane opened her narration. She recounted Basil's story, mentioning the food being taken aboard *Justice*, and the conflicting report of when Romeo meant to leave.

"He mentioned a week," Renfrew reminded her.

"The first fair breeze is what he told Basil—and there is a fine breeze tonight. I can sense the excitement in him. And why is he suddenly patching up all the family quarrels? That looks suspicious."

"You could be right, but what troubles you? I should think you, of all people, would be happy to see the back of him."

"He plans to take me with him. He as well as said so. I told him I wouldn't go, but he—he just doesn't *listen*, or hear. I think I should go home. Why risk being kidnapped?"

Renfrew's brow puckered in worry. "Your being at home wouldn't stop him, if that's what he has in mind. You have only a handful of servants at Catherine Street. Romeo might well have hired a band of men for the job. You'll be safer here, where I can watch you."

She felt a rush of warmth that he took the job on his own shoulders, but felt bound to object. "You can't stay with me all evening. As the host, you have other duties.'

"Mama must help us."

"She seems to think I am marrying Romeo," Jane said, and searched her companion for his reaction. That shadow in his eyes looked like frustration. "Why else did she sit me at his right hand for dinner? At least, I would have been at his right hand had she not served slaughtered animals."

"I'll explain the situation to Mama."

"You mean you've never told her!"

"Romeo had determined to leave England. You had determined not to have him. What was the point in precipitating another family quarrel? I thought it would be easier for all of us, mostly you, Jane, if we waited till the dust had cleared. Mama's temper is unsteady, and she is already at her wit's end with Romeo. In a few weeks, the whole tempest will be forgotten, and we can get on with it."

Jane heard all this with a joyous sense of incredulity. Renfrew's worried countenance told her what he had been going through. And with a growing knowledge of his peculiar family, she could well agree with his method of handling the situation. The only doubt in her mind was what a notorious flirt meant by "getting on with it." Did he mean a courtship, a wedding? Or did he mean no more than a flirtation? Uncertainty kept a rein on her pleasure.

"You tell your mother what you think is best, but I do think I should go home."

"No, not home. That's where he'll go looking for you. You're safe in a crowd. He'll hardly come in with pistols blazing and carry you off. And after the party, you can sleep here."

Jane considered this, but soon found an objection. "He'll be watching to see when I leave. If I don't—"

"He'll be watching the *carriage* leave. In fact, he'll probably try to abduct you from the carriage. That would be easier than to take you by main force from your house. Yes, that's when he'd do it. I'll accompany your aunt home. I suppose I'd best arm myself," he added unhappily. "Not that I'd actually use a pistol, but Romeo is afraid of firearms."

"Shall we tell your mother now?"

"You tell your aunt. I'll speak to Mama," he said, for he knew her first outburst would be strong. And it was. He had his mother called to the private parlor after Jane went in search of Mrs. Pettigrew.

"So that's what she is up to!" was the duchess's first reaction. "What a take-in. And here I have been lauding the chit's common sense. It was *you* Miss Halsey had in her eye all along. She goes beyond sensible; she is a sly hussy."

"It was not a scheme, Mama. Don't set your back up against Jane. The fault, if there is fault involved, is mine. I was often in her company along with Romeo, and came to realize by insensible degrees that she is the lady I wish to marry."

"Insensible is not the word, James. Nonsensical is closer to it. And now you think Romeo plans to kidnap her?"

"I'm afraid we must face the possibility."

"And he smiling and simpering at me like a Bath miss. 'Stitch up the rent in the family fabric,' he said. I'd like to stitch up his lips. Well, what is to be done, then? We cannot have him kidnapping Miss Halsey, I suppose."

"I have asked her to stay here overnight. Her aunt's carriage will proceed to Catherine Street. I fancy that is when Romeo will make his move. I'll be in the carriage and accompany him to the *Justice*. He has the ship all prepared to sail tonight. Let us try to make this evening as . . . normal . . . as possible."

"I'm glad you didn't say enjoyable. This is about as enjoyable as sitting on a powder keg with a torch at your feet. Your father is the wise one, staying in Hampshire. I shall leave in the morning whether Romeo kidnaps Miss Halsey or not."

"He won't succeed. I'll have the blue guest room prepared for Miss Halsey," James said, and escaped back to the ballroom.

The music proceeded from quadrille to country dances and waltzes. Mrs. Pettigrew was apprised of the plan and agreed to it. Jane was careful to remain near groups, and at the farthest possible distance from a doorway or window. After standing up with her once, Romeo did not pester her again. He danced with several ladies, including Belle. He capered, he preened, and insulted half the assembled company.

Lord Bathurst was taken to task for his mismanagement of the colonies. "You politicians are all alike. I resent that you have usurped a fine old Greek word, and debased it to a synonym for corruption."

"I'm not accustomed to receiving lectures from a young whelp."

"Age confers no distinction, sir. I may be a young dog, but you grow old like an ox. Your girth increases, but not your wisdom."

While Romeo sparred with politicians and flirted with the ladies, Renfrew found an opportunity to stand up with Jane for a waltz. "I spoke to Mama," he said.

"Yes?"

"You are to remain here overnight."

"Was she angry that I have declined Romeo's offer?"

"She was disappointed," he said vaguely, "but she'll get over it. Has Romeo tried to get at you?"

"No, he's hardly even glanced at me."

"That is an attempt to disarm your suspicions. He'd be trailing at your skirt tails if he weren't up to something. We won't let him out of our sight for a moment."

Romeo was one of the first to leave the rout. He took a formal leave of his mother and Renfrew. "I have an early day at Burlington House," he explained. "We are very busy there just now. I'll call on you before I set sail, Mama. Will you be in London?"

"I plan to leave very soon for Hampshire. But I shall remain a few days longer. Come tomorrow, Romeo."

"I shall be here, if the gods permit."

It was found highly suspicious that he placed a dry kiss on his mother's cheek, and shook James's hand not once but twice.

"I don't trust him an inch," his mother said, after he had gone capering out the door.

"Nor I. He'll get into his carriage and be lurking to watch when Jane leaves." Renfrew went to the door and saw that the carriage did go to the end of the block and turn the corner.

It seemed the auspicious moment to get the Halsey party into their chaise, while Romeo was not there to see exactly how many ladies and gentlemen entered it. Jane remained behind, while the others left, along with James, who stuck an unloaded pistol under his jacket.

Jane was too fidgety to remain at the dance, but didn't want to go to her room. She wanted to see Renfrew the instant he returned, and stationed herself in the small private parlor where she had spoken with him earlier. The duchess dropped in from time to time to talk to her.

"You must find us an odd sort of family," she said, shaking her head. "We had no intention of subjecting you to anything of this sort when we sicced Romeo on you, Miss Halsey. We merely thought a sensible gel like yourself could handle him. We ought to have armed you with a chair and a whip. The boy is unmanageable. I have come to see it now."

"He hasn't actually done anything—yet," Jane said forgivingly.

"Renfrew will make him toe the line. He's good at that."

"Yes, he seems ... capable," Jane said, and blushed for no discernible reason.

"I'd best return to my guests. What a waste of time. I could be home tending my roses."

"Ah, you have a rose garden! How I miss the roses at Halsey Hall. My mama loved her roses. She had three dozen varieties."

The duchess's interest perked up. "Had she indeed? I noticed your aunt had only one."

"Yes, and it planted in the shade. Queen Anne is hardy, but even she must have *some* sun." Jane nodded.

"You know a little something about roses, then?"

"I used to help Mama."

"Indeed!" The other guests were forgotten. The duchess sat down and said, "What did you do about those black spots? I don't mean that gray, powdery mildew ..."

"No, no. You mean the black spots that come after a rain. Mama used copper powder, but was not entirely happy with it, especially in a really damp spring."

"When do we ever have anything else? I swear the clouds watch for the buds to come out, then pour water on them to bring out the black spots. Sulfur is not much help either."

Lord Renfrew was astonished to find, upon his return, that his mother had forgotten all about Romeo, and had deserted her party to chat with Jane. She looked up with an air of annoyance at the interruption. "Well, did the young scalliwag attack the carriage?" she demanded.

"No, he didn't," Renfrew said, frowning in perplexity. "He didn't follow it at all. We purposely set a slow pace so he could find us, but he didn't show up."

"It is all a hum. He said he would come to see me tomorrow. He had best do it in the morning, for I am determined to return to Hampshire and try that fungus remedy you have been telling me about, Miss Halsey."

"I might as well go home, then, if I was mistaken about Romeo," Jane said uncertainly.

"No!" the duchess and Renfrew exclaimed at once.

"He might still make an effort for you at Catherine Street," Renfrew said.

"And I want to hear a little more about that grafting method your mama was trying, Jane. Sealing up the edges with paraffin sounds an excellent notion. But I shan't keep you two from the dance any longer. Run along and dance with Miss Halsey, James. I have been boring the poor girl to pieces with my chatter. You know how I get carried away." She waved them out the door.

Jane felt embarrassed at the bother she had caused, all, apparently, for naught. "I have created a tempest in a teapot," she admitted.

"The night isn't over yet," Renfrew countered. He placed his hand on her elbow as they walked along the corridor. Jane was minutely conscious of his touch as they walked along. "I mean to return to Catherine Street. I would have lingered, but I had a peculiar apprehension that Romeo would return here and carry you off."

"I wonder where he is."

"He's living on his ship. Presumably that's where

he went. I could take a spin down there and see if his chaise is around."

Jane looked a question at him. "I don't suppose— no, that would be unwise."

"What would?"

"For me to go with you. If all you're going to do is look for his carriage, I mean. You weren't planning to actually speak to him?"

Renfrew's fingers slid down her arm till he was holding her fingers. "No, it is only to drive down and have a look. Come with me. I have my trusty unloaded pistol, in case of trouble."

"And I shall bring my sharp eyes."

Laughing, they slipped out of the parlor and out the side door. The duchess saw them go, and nodded her head in approval.

Chapter Thirteen

RENFREW REALIZED when his carriage left the west end of London and entered the less polite purlieus of Holborn Road and Cheapside that he had erred to bring Jane along. He was not entirely easy in such a place after dark himself. The streets were ill-lit, if they were lit at all. What had possessed him to allow Jane to accompany him? It was unlike him to behave with so little thought to propriety.

Jane shivered into her pelisse and said in a small voice, "It's very dark in this part of town, is it not?"

He used it as an excuse to move to her banquette. His hand fumbled in the darkness and grasped her fingers reassuringly. "Gaslight hasn't yet made its way throughout the entire city. The East India docks neighborhood where Romeo's ship is anchored will be even worse. I can take you home, if—" Yet to take her home would involve a great loss of time, and to leave her at one of the taverns or decrepit inns dotting their way was obviously impossible.

"Oh, no! I am not afraid!" she exclaimed untruthfully, but Renfrew noticed her fingers were clutching at his.

"We must trust to luck and a good team to arrive without incident," he decided.

After a long drive and a few false turns, they finally reached their destination unharmed. The lap of black water against the docks sounded menacing. Any evil thing could lurk in the shadows of ships at rest. And the ships did all seem to be at rest. There was no stirring of seamen on the decks, no lights, no sound but the soughing of the wind and the lap of water.

"You stay in the carriage. I'll go down and scout out the *Justice*," Renfrew said.

"I'm not staying here alone!"

"My groom will remain with you."

"You can't go alone, James! Some cutthroat seaman might knife you and throw your body into the river. We'd never see you again." Jane clutched desperately at his hands as the likelihood of this peril sank in.

Renfrew swallowed the lump in his throat that rose at her graphic description and said, "It will just take a minute."

"You dare not go alone," the groom said, already climbing down from his perch.

"We'll all go," Jane announced.

After some argument, Renfrew exerted his authority and ordered John Groom to remain behind to guard Miss Halsey. He carefully closed the carriage door behind him before leaving. As soon as Renfrew had gone ten yards, Miss Halsey stuck her head out the window and ordered John Groom to go after him.

"I shall remain in the carriage with the doors locked," she said firmly. Not till the groom had crept away did she realize the carriage doors had no locks, so she slunk into the darkest corner to hide herself from any stray evildoer, and peered toward the docks. She felt suffocated from fear, but there was excitement burgeoning beneath it when she recalled Renfrew's concern for her safety. What was there to be afraid of? She hadn't felt so alive in months, maybe years. If she had to live the rest of her life in monotony, she would at least have tonight to remember.

Before Renfrew had gone far, he recognized Romeo's flag waving in the stiff breeze. All seemed quiet aboard. There were no lights, but only a guard, patrolling back and forth on deck. Many of the ships were protected in the same manner, presumably to prevent pillaging. The scene could hardly be more innocent. Obviously Romeo wasn't planning to leave that night.

When Renfrew was satisfied, he returned to the carriage. His groom managed to get back before him, and sat innocently on his perch when Renfrew entered the chaise.

"All's quiet," he said to Jane. "We've let our imaginations carry us away. I'll take you home."

It came as a disappointment to hear that the evening was over. "To Catherine Street, do you mean?"

"Oh, no, he might still make a try for you there. I wonder ... Let us take a spin past your house, just so we can rest easy in our minds."

The house on Catherine Street was all in darkness. No carriage lurked nearby. Renfrew even got out and went on foot all around the building, checking for ladders or open windows. He saw nothing suspicious.

"If he had made any attempt, the house would be in an uproar. He hasn't been here," Jane said.

"It looks that way," he agreed doubtfully, "yet the more innocent everything appears, the more I suspect one of his tricks. I wish I'd paid more attention to the various Grecian myths he is forever spouting."

"You think he's planning to attack later?" Jane asked.

"Possibly."

"That would be like Romeo, to lead us astray. He's really very ingenious, is he not? And reckless! Imagine, kidnapping Lady Barbara."

Renfrew heard the edge of approval in her voice, and felt a sting of jealousy. "A delightful stunt," he growled.

"We didn't see any sign of a carriage lurking about," she mentioned.

Renfrew gave a start of surprise, or discovery. "No, and by God we didn't see his carriage at the dockyards either. He wasn't there."

"The authorities wouldn't let him leave his carriage at the docks."

"He never pays any heed to authority. More delightful insouciance on his part. He complained to me the other night that someone entered his rig while it was waiting by the ship, so he hired a lad to sleep in it."

Jane sat a moment, puzzling. "Where is he, then? Would he have gone home, to Belgrave Square?"

"He said good night; he left. Why would he do that if he meant to sleep at home? Of course it's possible he's just—" He came to a conscious stop.

"What?"

"Just—out celebrating his final night ashore."

"With the local hetaerae?"

"That was my meaning," he said stiffly.

"That would occur to *you*, of course," she sniffed. "More likely he's at Burlington House, checking up on the Marbles. That is why he arrived late this evening. Basil says he's always there."

"He wouldn't be there at this hour. He couldn't even get in."

"He has his own key."

"Really?" James felt a little ripple of apprehension up his spine. This was beginning to sound like one of Romeo's obsessions, and when Romeo became obsessed, he was capable of any folly. It was obsession that led him to kidnap Lady Barbara. James had thought Athene was this month's obsession, but perhaps he was mistaken. He really hadn't pestered Jane that much. "If that's where he is, there's no need to worry, I suppose. He's just kissing the Marbles good-bye."

"He'd have to do it through layers of papers and canvas and wood. They're all wrapped up and ready to go to the museum," she informed him.

The ripple that still scampered along Renfrew's spine intensified. He tried to stave off believing the dreadful idea that had occurred to him. It was impossible, a project too large for one man. He'd have to gain access to Burlington House. "He has his own key." He had even overseen the packing. But he'd require a ship . . . something along the lines of a frigate, with the hold all carefully lined with cotton wool as an extra precaution. He'd make his move from Burlington House, closer to the Thames than the British Museum, and with fewer staff to hamper him. The Marbles were all carefully wrapped for transfer to the less accessible museum in a few days. And to further muddy the waters, Romeo would cause some confusion regarding the time of his departure. He wasn't waiting for the first fresh breeze after the Marbles were removed. He was leaving now, tonight.

"I'm a fool!" Renfrew sighed. "Please, tell me I'm wrong. He can't be—it isn't possible."

"What? Tell me, Renfrew."

"Romeo is planning to kidnap the Elgin Marbles."

"Don't be ridiculous!" she scoffed.

"But wait, *think* ridiculous for a moment. Think like Romeo," he added satirically. He briefly outlined the direction of his thoughts.

Once the idea was planted, it took root rapidly. It was so exactly like Romeo. "And I was just a—a red herring!" Jane exclaimed, offended to the core. "He never planned to kidnap me at all. It was all dust in our eyes."

"If it offends you, I'm sorry," he said in an unsteady voice.

"It was rather flattering, in a way," she admitted. "But he can't be doing it tonight, Renfrew. There was no action aboard the *Justice*."

"Don't vent your disappointment on me! You called me James before."

Such a telling speech had to be ignored. "In fact, he wouldn't have designed such a glaringly obvious flag if his hope was for secrecy," she continued. "I mean, the EIC frigates all look very much alike. That flag just calls attention to his ship."

"It calls attention to the ship that is flying the flag. Do you believe for one moment that was the *Justice*? I don't. He's moved the *Justice* to some convenient spot for taking the Marbles aboard. He had her homemade banner raised on a different ship, in case I went checking up on him. He's gulled us, Jane."

"Oh, dear, they'll put him in the Tower if he's caught."

Renfrew drew a long, deep breath and said, "How peaceful that would be."

"James! He would hate that medieval fortress! You must *do* something."

"Yes, yes, I'm thinking."

"What is there to think about, gudgeon?" she demanded sharply. "Go to Burlington House at once. We must stop him."

Renfrew's brows rose, and his nostrils dilated in anger. He had spent his mature years being fawned upon by the prettiest, most eligible ladies in England. To be ordered about in unvarnished phrases by a provincial miss was an entirely new experience for him. And to realize that the object of it all was to save his troublesome brother, of whom he was becoming thoroughly tired, was the last straw. He could not recall that any lady, even his mother, had ever called him a gudgeon.

"Well, what are you waiting for?" she asked.

His brows settled down, his nostrils relaxed, and a reluctant smile tugged at his lips. It was just as well Jane hadn't seen his sudden fit of pique. He yanked the checkstring and directed his groom to Burlington House. "Spring 'em," he urged, then turned to Jane. "You . . . forgot . . . to say please" was his only complaint.

"Pardon me. I didn't realize the Stapford family took any interest in etiquette."

"It seems one of us will have to change his tune."

The horses' pace quickened, and the smoothness of the ride deteriorated accordingly, till the occupants were being bumped around like turnips in a cart. The grating of the wheels over cobblestones and the clopping of hooves made conversation difficult.

"You realize he is leaving this very night," Jane called. "Basil said he was having fresh produce put aboard this afternoon. That is why he wanted to make up with you, and kiss his mother good-bye, the Judas."

Renfrew duly noted Jane's change of attitude. "That is very likely why he instituted this family quarrel in the first place. He wanted an excuse to get away from us, so we wouldn't be asking too many questions about his activities—all that money I forwarded to him. He mentioned having paid a thousand pounds in seamen's salaries. He's hired a band of brigands." He drew out his unloaded pistol and looked helplessly at it.

"Put that toy away," Jane ordered. "A pity there isn't time to round up Bow Street. However, I daresay you would prefer some discretion in the matter."

"That would be a pleasant change."

"You will have to try moral persuasion," she advised.

"I fear we follow different moralities, Romeo and I."

"It has been my experience that you differ more in the details of execution than the basic morality. You both *use* people, feign a—a regard you don't feel, to deceive an innocent—" She came to a stumbling halt.

"Is this a fish story? Are we speaking of red herrings and gudgeons? I hope you realize, Jane, that I had no intention of deceiving you. It all began innocently."

As Jane had no intention of revealing how deeply

his unintentional deception had wounded her, she was swift to change the subject. "We're nearly there," she said, as Burlington House loomed in the distance.

He took her hand and said softly, "I hope so, but I fear we still have a little distance to go, before you forgive me."

As the carriage thundered up to Burlington House, all seemed to be dark and silent. There was some sort of cortege—it looked like a funeral party—farther along the road, but it was not heading directly to the river by the shortest route, as Romeo would be doing. The cortege was lit by torches, too, which removed any air of stealth. A band of ragamuffin men behind were chanting some funereal hymn.

"What's that? Should we investigate?" Jane asked.

"There's no time. It looks like a burial train for paupers. They get little enough ceremony, poor devils. We'll go directly into Burlington House."

The front door was locked. "There should be a guard," Jane said. Renfrew banged on the door, trying to rouse him. "Hush! You'll only warn Romeo you're here. We'll have to climb in a window."

No window was conveniently left open. Renfrew removed his jacket, and with that to protect his hands and muffle the sound, he broke the closest window and clambered in.

"I'll stand watch out here," Jane said.

It wasn't more than a minute and a half before Renfrew returned, coming out the door. "The Marbles are gone," he announced, in a hollow voice.

"They were stored along the corridor . . ."

"I know where they were. He's got them."

"Perhaps the guard just decided to move them?"

she said doubtfully. It was only despair speaking, a reluctance to acknowledge the awful truth, and they both knew it.

"The guard hasn't moved anything but his elbow. He's drunk. A bottle of ouzo is on the floor beside him. That's a particularly vile brew Romeo brought back with him from Greece."

"He can't have gotten very far, Renfrew. He was at the party a few hours ago. The boxes would all have to be loaded on to wagons or something."

"His men might have been doing that while we danced. He arrived plenty late. I daresay he's already set sail."

"No, no. They would wait for darkness to fall," she said. "We left very shortly after him, and there was no sign of life at the dock. He isn't there yet. He is en route. He shouldn't be hard to find, dragging all those coffin boxes along. Oh!" They exchanged a meaningful look.

"That's it!" Renfrew said. "The funeral cortege—but it was headed the wrong way, to the west. He wouldn't have anchored the *Justice* west of the Isle of Dogs. The larger docks are all there, or east of there. No, he's only taking a circuitous route, in case I follow him. Let's go."

He took her hand and dashed back to the carriage. The groom heard his directions and whipped the team into action.

"You can never stop him. He had two dozen men," Jane pointed out. "You have only your groom—and me."

"And an unloaded pistol," James added, drawing it forth with a rueful glance. "Romeo won't be armed either, I shouldn't think. He despises firearms."

"Then it will have to be moral persuasion after

all—and the fear of God. Tell him what the consequences will be . . . how he will shame the family."

"He won't care a brass farthing about that. No, that won't do it . . . but I think I know what will," he added, with an anticipatory smile.

"What?" she asked eagerly.

The carriage slowed noticeably. James stuck his head out the window, and the groom called, "I see them half a block ahead. Shall I run right up against them?"

"No, stop here," James replied.

When the carriage stopped, he opened the door and got out. "Wish me luck, Miss Halsey."

She began to step down from the carriage. "What are you going to do?"

"Prevent disaster, if possible."

"James, he won't hurt you!"

"He'll certainly do his best."

"Oh—be careful!"

"Nonsense, I've been careful all my life, and where has it got me?" A reckless smile beamed, and he lowered his head for a quick, fierce kiss on her lips.

The whole night seemed unreal. This reckless streak in Renfrew was as unrealistic as the rest, and infinitely more exciting. She felt she was being kissed by a pirate, or highwayman. He didn't put his arms around her, but his lips clung, burning, to hers.

When he lifted his head, he said, "This way is much better, don't you think?"

Jane just stared mutely, wondering if she was dreaming the whole thing. Renfrew straightened his jacket, smoothed his cravat, and held the door for her to reenter the carriage.

She entered reluctantly, then he marched at a

quick pace toward the funeral cortege. Jane watched him a moment, then descended from the carriage and darted forward, accompanied by the groom, who, for the first time in a long and blameless career, left the carriage standing in the middle of the street unattended. She followed Renfrew to the very front of the cortege, past flat wagons loaded with coffins in a weird and nonhuman variety of sizes and shapes. Tarpaulins were thrown over them, but at close range the contours of the boxes could be discerned below.

The parade came to a halt, and she noticed the group of ruffians were drawing in a circle around their leader. By dint of elbowing and shoving, she managed to slink her way toward the front of the throng. There stood Lord Romeo, still in his evening clothes. He wore a cocky, jeering expression on his pretty face. He reminded Jane of a young bantam cock, facing a sober rooster.

"So, brother, you have followed my trail." Romeo laughed. "Much good it will do you, but still I congratulate you. You are not quite so obtuse as I thought."

"Nor you quite so clever as you thought, whelp."

Romeo bridled up at the demeaning term. "Had I realized I had a less unworthy opponent, I would have taken greater precautions. You have been to the docks, and to Burlington House, I expect?"

"I have admired both your flag, flying on whatever ship you chose for the charade, and your rather hackneyed trick of getting the guard drunk."

"It was so obvious I could hardly believe the fellow went for it. Imagine, trusting a Greek bearing gifts. I fear my little joke was lost on him. Perhaps if I'd made it a wooden horse . . ."

"This affair won't be viewed as a joke, Romeo.

Take the Marbles back. *Now.* You can do it before daylight."

"By dawn, I shall be afloat, returning Athens' heritage to its homeland. I tried to do it by peaceful means. You know I offered to buy the Elgin Marbles, and was laughed out of the House. You can't make an Englishman see justice. He is too busy worrying about laws."

"You know you're in the wrong, Romeo. The Marbles were bought and paid for."

"I'd rather be wrong with Plato, than right with such men as Elgin and Bathurst."

"You haven't a chance of getting away with it. Every ship in the navy will be after you."

"I am prepared for that contingency. The *Justice*—you realize now the significance of the name?—is armed and manned. Like a Lacedaemonian, I ask not how many the enemy are, but where they are, that I might extinguish them."

"First you'll have to extinguish me. And this secret dart under cover of darkness doesn't look much like a wish for confrontation. Quite the contrary."

Romeo looked around, unfazed. "I see your army is limited to John Groom and a girl. Oh, it is you, Athene!" He smiled and bowed. "But if you think to bribe me with Miss Halsey, I fear you are wide of the mark, James. I have begun to find her rather dull and unimaginative, you know. Is that all the inducement you have brought? I am surprised at the paucity of your attack. Even a mouse knows better than to trust its success to one hole." He gave a leap of alarm. "The *Justice*! You've scuttled her! By God, I shall never forgive you for this, James. That is foul play, to sneak down to Woolwich and sink my ship."

"Is that where she's anchored? I thank you for

the information." Renfrew nodded to his groom, who turned and fled.

Jane assumed he was taking some precaution to see the ship was incapacitated. She watched as Romeo flew into a childish tantrum.

"That was contemptible, taking advantage of my moment's agitation." Over his shoulder he ordered a few of his men to stop the groom. "We might bandy words all night, or we might settle this dispute like gentlemen. Why should whole armies suffer and die? It shall be just you against me, James, man to man, till one of us falls."

A wicked smile gleamed in Renfrew's eyes. He bowed ceremoniously. "My thoughts exactly. But let us settle the terms of victory. If I win, you return the Marbles to Burlington House."

"*When I* win, you allow me to leave without making any report to the authorities. A clean getaway. Agreed?"

"Agreed."

They shook hands.

Jane felt a knot of fear grow within her. What were they going to do? Was it to be a duel? Romeo despised firearms, but perhaps swords . . . In an instant she saw a mental vision of Renfrew, bleeding on the ground, and felt weak with terror. She wanted to object, but fear held her rigid.

Chapter Fourteen

ROMEO AND Renfrew stood facing each other. Each wore an implacable face. Jane discerned the family resemblance as she studied them. Both were handsome, but Romeo looked a smaller caricature of James, a sort of parody.

"Strip to your girdle then, and let the contest begin," Romeo said.

"I don't wear a girdle."

"Nor I. We shall fight naked, in the Grecian style. Upright, or pancratium? As I have the advantage of you in practice, I give you the choice."

Jane frowned in confusion. It was soon obvious Renfrew shared her uncertainty.

"I don't know what you're talking about," he said.

"Pancratium—all strength."

"That suits me, but I refuse to strip to the buff."

"No matter. We have no oils for a rub, nor fine sand to optimize our hold. We'll fight in our trousers, then. Three falls, both shoulders to the ground, win. No biting or gouging. Otherwise, anything goes."

Wrestling! They were going to wrestle to decide the matter.

"Where do you want to do it?"

Romeo looked around the dark street. "Here."

"Here? In the middle of the road?"

"It will be hard falling, but at least there's no traffic at night. My men will form a ring. They've done it often enough before. I warn you, James, I am in fighting trim." He uttered a low laugh, and began stripping off his jacket, shirt, and evening slippers.

Renfrew did likewise. Jane stood mesmerized, feeling she was watching something not only highly irregular and definitely in questionable taste, but possibly even immoral. She had never before seen a man undress. Her eyes, glowing with interest, flickered from Romeo to Renfrew, measuring the physique of each. Romeo was small, but he was well-muscled, and as lithe as a cat. Renfrew was larger, also well-muscled, but he lacked Romeo's agility. She looked with considerable interest at the patch of dark hair curling on his chest, and felt a strange quiver inside.

"Ponce Sykes shall decide the outcome, if that meets with your approval?" Romeo said. An uncouth man in fustian stepped forth from the crowd. "He is one of my students, and is familiar with the rules," Romeo explained. James nodded his acceptance.

A shout rose up from the throng, the combatants bowed formally, and were immediately locked in battle. It began tamely enough by each man gripping the other, first by the upper arms, then around the waist. In this manner they grappled together a moment. The throng were all for Romeo, and their shouts led Jane to fear that, though small, he was a past master of this arcane art.

"He'll have no trouble. He dropped Bull Billings three times in the space of two minutes," one remarked, laughing, "and Bull weighs twenty stone."

"Aye, the wee lad's a proper man of science. See how he uses his legs as a lever. There goes John Bull to the ground. Sounds like he cracked his head open." A roar of approval filled the night.

Jane looked in horror as Renfrew was thrown to the ground. Romeo had tripped him in some cunning manner from behind. He moved so quickly she had not seen the exact maneuver, but she saw with awful clarity that Renfrew was temporarily stunned. His head hit the cobblestones with a dreadful bump, and he lay inert a moment, while Romeo threw himself on top, holding his shoulders to the ground. Ponce bounded forward and examined him. "One fall for Lord Romeo!" he called. Romeo stood triumphantly over his victim, with his arms raised over his head, acknowledging the throng's ovation.

While he was still mincing about, Renfrew stuck his foot between Romeo's legs, and ere long the smaller, too, was on the ground. James leapt on him and held his shoulders down.

"That was a low stunt, James!" Romeo exclaimed. "But not illegal in pancratium. I daresay I would have resorted to something similar in extremis. That is a point for my opponent, Ponce." Ponce announced the score.

The combatants did not immediately rise from the ground, but rolled and tumbled about there till they were covered in dust. Sometimes one was on top, sometimes the other. The scene reminded Jane of a squirrel fighting a dog. Though smaller, Romeo was so frisky it was like trying to catch mercury. He seemed to squirm out of any grip James managed to get on him. After a few moments struggle, Romeo came out on top. Ponce pounced in and called, "That's two points for Lord Romeo!" and another cheer went up.

"It is not!" Jane exclaimed, and bounded into the middle of the ring. "Why do you give him a point? They're both on the ground!"

"Lord Renfrew is pinned. See how his shoulders both touch the earth. That is a point for Lord Romeo."

"But he's sitting on Renfrew's head! That cannot be fair!"

"Those are the rules, milady."

"Romeo's shoulders were pinned a minute ago! I saw it very clearly. Why did you not give Renfrew a point then?"

"Only one shoulder was pinned."

"Go away, Jane," Romeo said coolly. "In days gone by, I, too, have lain in the dust, but now let me win noble renown."

"It's unfair! Everyone's on your side."

A torrent of boos and "shame" rose up around her, and when Jane saw that Renfrew was not seriously harmed, she retired sulkily from the ring. The gentlemen both rose up on their feet and began circling each other warily. Romeo tried a repetition of his old tripping stunt, but Renfrew was wise to him this time. He caught Romeo's leg with his long arm and flung his brother into the air. As soon as Romeo hit the ground, James pinned his shoulders down and won a point.

Romeo smiled up in approval. "Victory shifts from man to man. This is a more interesting match than I anticipated. Now we are even again. Two all. Next fall is victory—for one of us." He uttered a confident laugh and pulled himself to his feet.

The mood quickened. Jane felt her heart pounding, and at one point noticed with shock that she was clinging to the arm of a total stranger, and a very rough-looking spectator he was, too. When the crowd cheered for Romeo, she shouted as loud as she could, to drown them out and encourage Renfrew.

Both men were beginning to show some fatigue by the last bout. With increased caution, they took their time, circling, looking for advantage, wary of a sudden attack. When Romeo made his move, it was so swift and unexpected, James didn't even see his leg flash out. He only knew he was suddenly flying through the air, and if his head hit that cobblestone, he was done for. The Elgin Marbles were done for. Romeo was done for. He'd be arrested, and quite possibly beheaded as a traitor. With the speed of desperation, he flung out his arms and broke his fall with his hands. His right arm took the force of the fall. A sharp pain flew up his arm. If a bone wasn't broken, he would be much surprised. And how the devil could he hope to win against his skillful brother with one wing broken? Romeo came prancing around, strutting like a cock.

Renfrew began to rise up painfully. As he rose, Romeo came closer, laughing. Renfrew was not only angry, but humiliated to be beaten in front of Jane. His greater size made victory appear certain, but he was unfamiliar with these Grecian conjuring stunts, and knew he couldn't outmaneuver his brother. The blood throbbed in his head, and the pain from his arm made him nauseated. He knew that in a boxing match, he could flatten the boy in one second. If it was anything goes, he'd switch from wrestling to boxing. As he rose, he drew his left arm back, and when he gained his balance, his arm shot out. His fist caught Romeo on the side of his jaw and lifted him six inches off his feet. He fell to the cobblestones in a surprised heap. Renfrew leapt on him and pinned his shoulder down.

Ponce darted forward and examined the situation. "Three falls, and the victor is Lord Renfrew!" he announced. He took Renfrew's right arm, and a howl louder than the rest of the onlookers combined came out of Renfrew's mouth.

"Watch it," he growled. "I've busted a wing."

"You're a game scrapper, milord. A bruiser I'd say, from that left."

"How's Lord Romeo?"

They both bent over to examine him. Jane was suddenly there, too, laughing and crying as Renfrew drew her to him with his good arm. Romeo's eyes fluttered open, and he smiled up vaguely from the ground. "I hear music, James. The music of the spheres. Am I dead? How lovely it is—though my jaw hurts like the devil." He rubbed it tenderly as he looked around. "I see no sign of the fire and brimstone Vicar has been trying to convince me of." He turned to Jane, then back to Renfrew. "Ah, yes, now I recall. And James actually beat me. Incredible! I see you know how to win a victory, James, but not how to make gain of it. Winner take all. To the victor go the spoils." He waved his arm invitingly toward the lady.

"In that case . . ." Renfrew pulled Jane into his left arm, and she went happily. It seemed a moment out of time, in some other strange land, to see Renfrew and Romeo, half-naked and covered in dirt, their hair tousled and their faces grimed. The grinning, raucous circle of faces around them were no more out of place than the rest. And in any case, when she closed her eyes, they disappeared. James's lips were hot on hers. The heat of his body entered through her silk gown to warm her heart. A flame leapt inside her as his lips moved hungrily, and he crushed her against him.

It was Romeo who pulled them apart. He had risen, and with one hand on each, he gently tugged till he had interrupted their embrace. "I shall temporarily provide the small rock necessary to hold back the wave of desire rising between you two," he explained. Jane opened her eyes and gave a guilty gasp of shock.

"I knew there was fire within you," Romeo accused. "It seems I was not the proper flint to strike it. You have got a wolf by the ears, James. How I envy you the task of taming her."

Renfrew shook himself back to attention. "I shan't insult your honor by inquiring whether you mean to keep your bargain, Romeo. We have only to settle the how of it."

"Certainly, dear boy, but I must say a word to my crew. High thoughts deserve high language, and I must appease them with some elocution—a duty I enjoy, and do particularly well." While he arranged torchlights to illuminate him, he hastily scoured his mind for crumbs of Sophocles and other scholars to bedazzle his audience. He went to the caravan and stood on top of the highest carton, where he struck a dramatic pose, clenched hand on naked breast, and torches carefully lighting him from both sides. What a picture it would make, when he had time to execute it. He was considerably astonished to hear a paraphrase of that barbarian Shakespeare come spontaneously from his lips. But he was happy to observe that he was in excellent voice. His words reverberated on the night air.

"Friends, soldiers, countrymen! Great goals are fought at great risk. We have fought a brave battle, men, but it is not possible to fight beyond our strength." There was a roar of approval. "Nobly to live, or nobly to die, and tonight you have all been ennobled by your striving for justice. I have struck a bargain with the enemy, the honorable enemy," and he bowed punctiliously to his brother. "I shall cleave to my word. The Marbles will be returned, but remember, friends, the army that retreats in order may fight again."

Renfrew felt a tremor of apprehension at that phrase.

The orator continued. "That wise counselor, time, decrees this is not the hour, but soon we shall return. Meanwhile, we suffer man's greatest agony: to have knowledge of right, but not power to execute it. Back to Burlington House posthaste, and thence to the *Justice*, where we shall deliberate this important matter when we are all thoroughly drunk."

This received the loudest cheer of all. With the promise of free-flowing wine to come, the men were not tardy to turn the wagons about and return the Marbles. Romeo oversaw the reversal of the wagons, and while this was going forth, Renfrew got dressed again.

Jane noticed his limp wrist. "Renfrew, you're hurt! Oh, I hope it is not broken!"

She was tying his cravat around his wrist when Romeo came to take his leave. "Gray-eyed Athene, you fill another of your historical roles—nurse of men. I came to shake hands, James, but I see I have maimed you. I trust it is not too painful. No hard feelings. It was a Cadmean victory, was it not? I suffered defeat of a principle, and you have suffered a physical wound. Your wrist hangs limply, like Spiro's after I broke it. It will mend in time. I have not been unacquainted with misfortune before, but I daresay it is the first time you have been wounded. You wrestled excellently, by the by. I did admire that left. We do not think alike, but we are brothers still, and I have come to appreciate some latent talent in you."

Renfrew bowed and said "Thank you."

Romeo returned the bow. "You're welcome, James. I do not sprinkle compliments lightly. If only your mind were as well tuned as your body. A wise old Greek once said 'The blood around men's hearts is their thinking,' and your blood has congealed in this climate. I do not hold you responsible for your reprehensible defense of England's thievery. Where is the justice in a rich man buying a poor man's children? Speechless, I see. I must join my men on the *Justice*."

"Will you be returning to Greece?"

"Soon, but perhaps a quick trip to Taunton first. I have not had a woman in—why are you *poking* at me, James?" James cast an apologetic glance at Jane, who shook her head ruefully.

"You'll come home and see Mama first?" James asked.

"Yes, and perhaps Uncle Rufus. He is a director of the British Museum, is he not?" he asked nonchalantly.

James scowled. "He is, and so am I!"

"Pity. When will you and Jane be undertaking your honeymoon?"

"Very soon *after* you leave for Greece."

A light laugh fell from Romeo's lips. "You must not wait on my pleasure. Jane looked quite impatient when she was throwing herself at you. I shall leave now, and let you two ride passion's wave to the crest. How I envy you."

He left and, true to his word, returned every piece of marble on the wagons to Burlington House. He was happy he had had the foresight to put Thalia's head on board *Justice* that afternoon before the remove, however. James—poor, dull James—had said nothing about returning the spoils of any prior pilfering.

Renfrew shook his head in chagrin as he watched his brother depart. "I had hoped to sweep this under the carpet, but I really must warn them at the British Museum. Are you quite sure you're up to having Romeo as a brother-in-law?"

"I shall not give that any thought till I have an offer of marriage, sir!"

James looked astonished. "Didn't I ask you? Forgive me, gray-eyed Athene. My brother's arrogance has worn off on me."

"As well as a *little* of his daring." She smiled approvingly.

James frowned. "Miss Halsey, will you do me the honor to marry me?"

Unhappy with such a blunt proposal, Jane demurred. "I fear your mother expects you to make a better match."

"She's gaining a gardening companion: what more could she want?"

"A title."

"She already has one."

This studied piece of obtuseness made Jane lose her temper. "This is not the way *Romeo* proposed!"

"Comparisons, Miss Halsey, are odious."

She was prevented from replying by the assault of his lips. All thoughts of Lord Romeo slid from her mind as his bruising kiss deepened. Without verbal affirmation, it was understood she accepted his offer. A genteel young lady did not allow herself to be embraced so thoroughly in a public street, even at night, without marriage being understood.

They met John Groom returning with the carriage. "I left a couple of Runners at the *Justice*. She's at Woolwich, as he said. Bristling with guns and men. All that weight would account for his stripping the cabins, I daresay. The Runners didn't try to go aboard. It looks like you'll have to call in the army."

"Thank you, but it won't be necessary. We won," Renfrew said. His eyes caressed Jane. "Let us drive to Hyde Park to see the sun come up. A hero requires a touch of maudlin romance, I think?" They climbed into the carriage, fatigued but happy.

The eastern horizon was tinged with rose when they reached the park. During the trip, Renfrew had apologized for his brother, explained again his reasons for not courting Jane sooner, and apologized for having brought her along on such an unsavory outing. She had tried to explain away her own farouche behavior during the trip and particularly at the wrestling match.

"It was so strange, like a fever in the blood," she said, trying to understand it herself.

"There's a touch of the hot-blooded Greek in you, too." He smiled. "I believe I've picked up the taint as well. I thoroughly enjoyed the evening. I'm not even sure I did the right thing to prevent Romeo. There is something to be said for his point of view. Is it morally right for a rich nation to buy a poorer one's cultural heritage for money?"

She stared. "Renfrew! Don't even *think* it!"

"No, no. I'm not. Though, as a director of the museum—and I'm quite sure I could talk Uncle Rufus around, if you could have a word with Herb."

"His name is Basil. Good gracious, I thought I was marrying the sane one!"

"Where'd you get that idea?" He laughed, and pulled her into his arms for a kiss that was quite madly delicious.

It was ten-thirty the next morning when Lord Renfrew brought Jane back to Catherine Street. The engagement ring on her finger was a silent testimony to the duchess's approval of the wedding. She had urged Renfrew to get a ring on Jane and send the announcement to the papers that very day, before Romeo cut up any more larks to distract them.

Mrs. Pettigrew espied the carriage and Jane's smiles from the front window. Jane had landed herself a marquess, then. Any amount of good might trickle down to Basil from that connection. Abovestairs, Belle was busy preparing a gown for her afternoon outing with Sir Dabney Porter. She was drawn to the window by the sound of the carriage.

"Look, Munch," she called, and Munch came running. "Jane is laughing. They have managed to thwart Romeo's plan somehow."

"She's taking hold of his arm as if she owned it," Munch added. "She would never do *that* if he hadn't offered for her."

"See how she glows," Belle sighed, as the couple drew closer. "I bet they were kissing in the carriage. I shall ask her when she comes in."

Munch turned a condemning eye on her charge. "That you'll not, miss. There's times in life when human beans want a touch of privacy. And it looks like this is one of them," she added, as James bestowed a quick kiss on Jane's ear. Miss Munch watched as eagerly and as happily as her charge.